MANIA

LUCAS MANGUM

Madness Heart Press

June 2020

"MANIA - Revised Edition" © 2020 Lucas Mangum

Cover art © 2016 George Cotronis

Cover Design © 2020 by Lucas Mangum

ISBN: 978-1-522073-88-8

This new edition is for Mom.

Foreword

Our dreams come from a haunted place, the corporeal territory of our subconscious, a town which has reenacted our familiar, occult psychodramas for more than a century. I'm talking, of course, about Hollywood.

A friend and I visited that storied place this past February to see another friend who was battling some health issues. On our way to a haunted escape room, we ended up on the Walk of Fame. I took a picture of Jimi Hendrix's star to send my dad, saw someone walking a black goat, and got approached by too many panhandlers to count. All in all, the Walk was kind of gross. It should've been a demystifying experience.

But for some reason, it wasn't.

On multiple occasions that weekend, I glimpsed the Hollywood sign from the back of a Lyft and found myself feeling strangely wistful. That sign and the place it represents is so embedded in the collective unconscious of our nation, it's impossible to not feel *something* when seeing it in person, even from a distance.

Like most people I know, I grew up on movies.

First, they were a part of what made my childhood magical. I watched, awestruck, as Kirk Douglas and James Mason battled a giant squid, marveled at the space battles in the original *Star Wars* trilogy, and cowered under an attacking T-Rex all three times I caught *Jurassic Park* in the theaters. I had every movie from the Universal Monsters collection on VHS and wore out every tape. I repeatedly rented titles like *Tremors*, *Jaws*, and Stephen King's *It*. It was all pretend, but somehow also *real*.

Then, after experiencing the trauma of my parents' divorce, movies became a source of solace. The destruction of notable landmarks by alien invaders in *Independence Day* struck a shocking parallel to what I felt was a true loss of innocence. Childhood was over and watching the world end proved strangely cathartic. Action heroes as portrayed by Arnold Schwarzenegger and Jean-Claude Van Damme controlled their environments, just as I so desperately wished to control mine.

In my late teens, I entertained the idea of becoming a filmmaker myself, especially as I discovered lower budget offerings such as the countless Italian zombie movies, slasher films, and the output of Lloyd Kaufman's Troma Team. Making films like these seemed more within my grasp than, say, *Starship Troopers*. Of course, I learned very quickly that even the lowest of low budget features require more work than I cared to put in at the time. They also require a director with an uncanny ability to rally people behind their cause, to work for no money on something that may never see the light of day.

Books are easier. If no one cares about something I write, I'm the only one who cries. Failure as a filmmaker means letting down too many others.

But still, movies *haunt* me.

That's because movies are haunted.

They are our modern myths. They are how we come to understand the world. They're how we learn about love, about death, and how to laugh about both.

It's because they are haunted by *us,* just as we are haunted by them.

With *Mania*, I wanted to put the sort of film I wanted to make into book form. To some degree, I like to think I succeeded. *Mania* is an old school Hollywood ghost story inspired in equal parts by haunted media tales like *Ringu* and John Carpenter's *Cigarette Burns*, and by illuminati sex-cult conspiracy theories. For better or worse, and I suppose that's a matter of taste, the book's critics say it reads like a movie. I suppose if you're looking for a deep, immersive novel, you may be disappointed. However, if you're like me and you like your reads fast-paced and cinematic, you may find a lot to love here.

Although this is a new edition, not a whole lot has changed with the text itself. With the help of the inimitable Lisa Lee Tone, I've fixed some errors. I've also added this introduction and a short story called "Hollywood Blood and Guts," which continues *Mania*'s story and hopefully sets up further books in a satisfying way.

If you enjoy this book, feel free to let me know either by leaving a review on Amazon or by dropping me a line over at lucasmangum.com. Those personal notes sometimes mean more to me than any number of stars you can give.

I'm writing this while the world is still in the midst of the COVID-19 pandemic. I hope that by the time you're reading this, things have settled down some and we're all a little healthier and happier. As for me, I'll be hard at work on another book.

As always, thank you for reading. Stay badass, Mangumaniacs.

-Lucas Mangum

Austin, TX 5/12/2020

Prologue

"Come on, man. Open this fucking door."

Brady Parker knocked until his knuckles throbbed. He jabbed the doorbell with the thumb of his other hand.

"Ashton, no one's heard from you in days. Everyone's shitting their panties. Ashton." Bang. Bang. Bang. "Don't make me knock down this door, man. I hate violence."

He stopped knocking, waited. Nothing.

Brady took a step back, raised his foot to kick in the door. He sighed, thought better of it, and dug into his pocket for his wallet. He found a credit card buried behind all the others, an Amex he hadn't used in years.

I can't believe I'm about to break in here like a petty crook.

He slid the card into the door jamb, fiddled with it. His hand slipped, knocking his throbbing fingers against the edge of the frame. One knuckle split open, and he yelped. The credit card dropped between his feet. He picked it up, went to try again. This time the door unlatched.

The stink wafted from the cracked door, seemed to suffocate him. His hand went to his mouth and nose. He gulped, tried to control his gorge. Bile singed the back of his throat.

"What the hell ..." He coughed, kept his hand over his face. "Ashton, you better not have killed yourself in there, you fucking pussy."

He pushed the door all the way open. The scene inside brought the sickness bubbling back up. Greasy barbacoa and sour margarita mix sprayed his shoes. The puke soaked through, drenched his socks in its warmth. He belched, almost threw up more.

Blood decorated the walls of the front room of Ashton Smith's house. Splashes of it created macabre, abstract designs. The name Marielle was written over and over, the phrase Mother of Ghosts painted on the ceiling in dripping crimson letters. Other symbols and words in a language he couldn't read were painted in the same hand, the same ink. Slashed couch cushions bled cotton. Broken, overturned furniture lay across the gouged and soiled floor. A shattered mirror hung over the fireplace. The pungent shit smell choked the air.

He tried to find the words. He cursed himself for not just sending the police. *Why the hell did I have to come over here myself?* The last few weeks had been one disaster after another, but this was the diarrhea frosting on a double shit cake.

Whatever this is.

He turned to leave, to go to one of the neighbors' houses and call the police. Nothing else he could do. Nothing else ...

A wet moan from somewhere in the house stopped Brady midstride. He tried to ignore the bloodied walls, checked for any kind of activity.

"Ashton?"

A soft whimper responded.

Brady put his hand over his mouth and nose again and walked forward. The hot puke squished in his shoes. Rancid air filled his mouth. A dry heave jerked his body.

He crossed the living room, every instinct telling him to turn around and run away. Every instinct but that which propelled him forward, a primal need for knowledge, to slow down and look at the car accident, to try foods like scrapple, to pause horror movies during the grisliest death scenes. He trekked down the hallway.

Behind one of the doors, someone coughed. He balled one hand into a fist, wanted to say something tough, but spasms jolted his knees, and he could only manage a croaked variation of Ashton's name.

The person behind the door squealed. Brady pushed the door open and jumped back, braced himself against the wall. Between his shoulder blades, his shirt stuck to a bloody streak on the wall. He blubbered, tried to make words, tried to comprehend the sight in the bathroom.

It was Ashton, but there was little of the man left. Slashes covered his arms, legs, and naked torso. The shattered remains of the mirror showed cuts on his back. A bloody shirt concealed his nether regions like a diaper. Brady tried to meet Ashton's eyes. Two red, empty sockets stared back at him, weeping crimson tears.

Brady's whimpering synthesized into a singular high-pitched scream that didn't stop until the police came and dragged him out of the house.

One

The rain fell in sheets. Ward parked in front of a wrought iron gate topped with jagged spikes. On the other side, a cobblestone path cut through the woods up a steep hill. A large brick wall surrounded the rest of the property with stone gargoyles perched along the top like demonic sentries. The gate opened, and he drove forward, the wheels rattling against the cobblestone.

Trees thick with age lined the path. Their twisted, bare branches clawed at the heavens. The rain and darkness made it difficult to see, except when sheet lightning flashed and bathed everything in eerie, white light. In those moments, he could see more gargoyles positioned throughout the yard with angry, chiseled faces and cracked wings.

The hill plateaued into a courtyard with a large fountain, and the house stood like an old cathedral with spires that pierced the sky and a pointed arch over its front door. It reminded him of the set of a gothic horror movie, like the old Universal Pictures that he watched with his grandfather. Though Ward wrote, directed, and distributed films that reviewers called *loud and visceral*, his earliest influences were the campy effects and much tamer content of the 1930s and 40s horror movies. His grandparents had raised him, and it was because of his late grandfather that he had acquired his love of monsters, which had later evolved into a fascination with the truly monstrous human mind and its powers to create its own nightmares.

A light switched on and illuminated one of the stained glass windows, and the front door opened a crack, revealing the face of a man with thinning white hair. Ward got out of his car and followed the man inside.

The scent of old books and wood polish permeated the atmosphere. A human skeleton hung in a rusty birdcage by the door, and more petrified beasts stood along the dark hallway. Mr. Whale leaned on a cane with a silver wolf's head on the end of it. From what Ward had heard about the old man, he wouldn't have been surprised if the cane was a prop from the original Wolfman movie, but he didn't ask.

Whale pressed his lips together in something like a smile. "Can I get you anything?"

"Only what I came here for."

"Very well. You don't mind if I have a drink, do you? The storm is doing a number on my joints."

"Not at all."

Whale filled one glass from a decanter on a marble table and returned his attention to Ward.

"Follow me, William."

Mr. Whale led him into a room like a crypt for the cinematic dead. Film reels, ancient camera equipment, VHS tapes, storyboards, posters, and props were strewn about, hung on the wall, or stuffed into shelves. There appeared to be no real order, like the crypt was more of a mass grave.

"How do you find things down here?"

"There is a method, I assure you." Whale rooted through a shelf populated with books and folders.

Ward grunted in response.

Whale flung a couple of books onto the floor and muttered something to himself.

As he waited, Ward wished he had taken the old man up on that drink. He stuffed his hands in his pockets as Whale pulled a few folders out. Whale searched inside each one, shook his head, and tossed the folder aside, spilling pages across the floor. Ward worried he was wasting his time until he glanced up to see Theda Bara staring down at him from a poster of the lost film, *Salome*. Maybe coming here would be worthwhile after all.

When he turned to face Whale again, the old man held a large binder filled with the pages of what looked like a screenplay, but could've been a workplace manual. Whale's lips pressed together again in that almost-smile, as if that was all he could manage. He said, "I told you I'd find it."

Ward grabbed hold of the binder and opened it to the title page. "This is it?"

The old man didn't respond.

In Ward's hands, the screenplay seemed to hold no threat or mystical power. Its title, *Mania*, was the sole word on the front page. No author name. No one to contact for the rights. That made him question the veracity of the pages, but it also made sense. After researching the script, Jay had discovered that no one owned the rights to it anymore. No one even knew who had written it.

"*Mania*," Whale said. "The infamous, cursed screenplay."

"I don't believe in curses, but I'll take the hype."

Whale's lips spread, finally showing his teeth in a reptilian grin, and his eyes became two bright spots in a face that was old, withered, and otherwise drained of light.

"I knew your father," he said.

"That makes one of us." Ward tucked the binder under his arm and pulled out his checkbook. "Who do I make the check out to?"

"Object d'art Collectors."

Ward wrote the check and handed it to Mr. Whale. As the old man wrote out a receipt, Ward asked, "So how do you find all this shit?"

"A variety of ways."

"How did you find *Mania*?

"I'd rather not say." His eyes went a shade darker.

"Guess I'm out of luck if it's not the real thing."

"I can assure you that it's genuine."

"For what I'm paying, it better be."

"Ah, but how would the world know?"

"They know part of the story. Enough of it, anyway, from the last time it went into production."

"I see. Well, it's certainly real. You'll get your money's worth."

His money's worth. *What does that even mean?* A new film to reclaim his status as a cult director? A whole lot of hype and no payoff? He was certain that he wouldn't end up dead or crazy.

A cursed screenplay. What a load of shit.

Two

Rachel Katayama sat on the stoop outside her trailer, smoking a cigarette and looking up at the moon. Partially obscured by the clouds, it hung in the sky like a spectral orb while Altern8 played from her iPod dock. She slushed her foot around in the muddy earth and took in the smell of fallen rain. It had stopped an hour ago, but its damp scent still lingered in the air.

She went into her purse and brought out her phone. There was a message from William. Three words: "I got it."

She held the cigarette in her mouth as she typed: "Fucking awesome! I'm so excited for you."

"Us," he replied. "You, of course, have a part in it."

Rachel went to type a reply when footsteps sloshing through the mud announced the arrival of Dalton Carver, her A-list costar. Already cleaned up from the shoot, he now wore blue jeans, a polo shirt, and the smile that had won the hearts of numerous viewers. Dalton was the definition of a star: two to three films a year, modeling gigs in between.

"Hey," he said. "Feeling antisocial?"

Rachel smiled up at him. "Just needed some time to decompress."

"Is that what the cigarette's for?"

"Just a nasty habit."

"Especially for a pretty girl like you."

She hummed indifferently.

"So, what's a pretty girl like you doing sitting all alone?"

"Like I said, decompressing." She took a drag from her cigarette and deliberately blew the smoke in his direction. "What's a hot shot A-lister doing hitting on a working girl like me?"

"Come on, Rachel, don't be so hard on yourself."

"Well, they did let me have a trailer this time." She slapped her hand against its metal siding.

"I can't remember not having a trailer."

She blew more smoke toward him in hopes it would repel his advances. "Must be nice."

"Ah, it's okay; not all it's cracked up to be."

"Really?"

He laughed and said, "Okay, it's fucking sweet."

"Hmm." Rachel butted her cigarette and got to her feet. "Well, I have to get going. It's been fun working with you."

"Sure, sure." He ran his hand across his wavy, salt-and-pepper hair and turned away. She picked up on the calculated gesture to make himself seem only moderately interested. "Maybe you want to grab a drink?"

"I better not. I've got to get home."

"Oh, come on. It's just one drink. Besides, we just wrapped."

She walked past him.

"Hey, Rachel, it's on me, huh?"

"I have my own reasons to celebrate." She held up her phone. "I just got my next role."

Dalton threw his hands up. "What? In your boyfriend's next movie? You can celebrate that anytime." He shrugged and gave a cute, pleading expression.

Boyfriend. Was that how she defined her and Bill's relationship? She saw them as a lot of things: business partners, roommates, friends, and, yes, lovers. But a status like boyfriend and girlfriend sounded too childish to her, and they weren't married, nor were there any plans to get hitched that she knew about.

She did love him. She was sure of that much.

William had given Rachel her first American film role after discovering the short films she wrote, directed, and starred in overseas. He had given her a role in a film that nearly killed him, and she had been there to help him pick up the pieces afterwards. They had been through so much together that calling him a mere "boyfriend" seemed almost insulting.

Still, with a guy like Dalton making advances, considering herself spoken for might not be a bad idea. She smiled and said, "I do appreciate the offer, but yes, I've really got to get home to my boyfriend."

"Is one drink really going to hurt? Home will be there when you're done. He'll be there when you're done."

"Well, I admire your persistence anyway."

"What can I say? I didn't get as far as I did by taking no for an answer."

"How about this: we can go out for a drink sometime soon, but not tonight. One drink. That's all, and it has to be purely professional. If I get the wrong vibe from you, even if it's only my own paranoia, I'm going to get up and leave. If you try to follow me, I'll kick you in the balls. Got it?"

He pressed his lips together and nodded. His cheeks flushed a shade of red. "Fair enough."

She walked away from Dalton feeling good about the interaction. She wanted him to know up front that she saw them as nothing more than colleagues. Friends, at the most. One drink, later this week, wouldn't hurt. But tonight was out of the question.

Tonight, William needed her.

● ● ●

The first time Rachel had spoken to William had been on the phone. She had just released a DVD of her short films called *One Woman's Hell: The Short Films of Rachel Katayama*. He had been so taken by the content that he had called her to express his appreciation and to offer her a role in his second film.

As a fan of *Atrophy*, she had been floored that someone of William's caliber would even notice her work. At the time, she had only a professional interest in him. Their relationship didn't take a romantic turn until they met in person. Nothing turned Rachel on more than passion, which Ward had exuded at the time, and it wasn't long before she had started spending nights at his apartment in Hollywood.

He introduced her to all his friends in the industry, gave her advice when she asked for it, and took advice from her in order to get a different perspective on his work. They were partners, friends, and lovers, everything she wanted in a relationship.

As she left the set of *Black Reckoning*, she meditated on all of this. The new script would be their first direct collaboration in five years, and eagerness to work with him bubbled up inside her. Despite their relationship and all its ups and downs—and there were downs, especially in the emotional fallout after his last production—she still considered herself a fan. His work was important to her, and to have a part in it made her feel like she was a piece of something crucial.

She picked up speed, anxious to get to him and musing on the concept of a cursed script. While she had encountered her share of people who believed in curses and the supernatural, she didn't count herself among them. Most things attributed to the otherworldly could be explained away as psychological phenomenon, or in the more unfortunate cases, con artists exploiting people's hopes and fears to make a quick buck.

But a real curse?

Those only existed in the movies.

●●●

Ward sat in his study, surrounded by shelves packed with movie scripts, DVDs, and books. Just above his computer monitor hung a poster of *Atrophy*, the title spelled out in the gray roots of a dead tree. Human faces lined the trunk, mouths frozen in screams.

He stared down at the last page of the script, utterly captivated by its story: an abused teenaged girl runs away to Hollywood, dreams of stardom filling her head, only to be betrayed and murdered by her movie director lover.

He could film it, but something about it hurt him. He identified too strongly with the lead and her absent father, her psychologically wounded mother. His last film, *The Mouth of Hell*, had also been a largely personal project, and working on it had gouged him deeply, dragged him to the brink of suicide. Had it not been for Rachel, he couldn't say for sure if he would still be alive today.

He hoped she would be home soon.

He tried to keep his reservations at bay, but reading the screenplay had made him feel especially vulnerable. As if some wound buried deep under years of scar tissue had reopened while he experienced the protagonist's story.

He hardly knew his father. Stephen Ward had won Academy Awards. He had called his films his children. Not Ward, not his brother, Lance. Ward's mother had tried to kill herself in front of them once. She had tied a belt around her neck and dangled from the living room ceiling fan. Lance had held her legs while Ward called for an ambulance.

He looked up from *Mania* and sighed. It gave him chills to think about the story. Though on the surface it was unlike anything he had directed before, it deeply affected him. Reading it had drained him because he had wanted to see the actress, unnamed in the script, be successful and triumph in the end. It was a crime that she hadn't.

He tried to put it out of his mind, but the sadness and exhaustion came back even stronger the more he tried to avoid it. Like someone he loved had died.

The front door jerked open and snapped him out of his thoughts.

"Bill?" Rachel said. She was the only one who called him that. Her voice could hardly contain its excitement.

He came out into the living room to meet her.

"Hey," he said. "How was the last day of shooting?"

"Never mind that! How's the script? Have you read it yet?"

"It's something, all right."

"Yeah?"

"It's really different from much of what I've done, but in many ways, it's a film after my own heart. I kind of wish I could find whoever wrote it."

"So you're going to do it?"

"I think so." Ward petted Rachel's dark hair and curled the red streak in it around his finger. "Hell, I know so. While I was talking about it, and even after I had acquired it, I wasn't sure. I mean, what if it sucked? Now, having read it, I can't imagine not doing it."

Rachel touched his face and said, "You're so hot when you get fatalistic."

"Oh, I bet." He smiled at her, trying to bury his fears deeper.

"We should celebrate," she said. "Good things are ahead."

He wondered if that was true.

Three

She wakes from sleep deeper than death.

Dormant since the last calling, she hungers for sustenance.

The life force.

The faith.

The fear.

Not yet strong enough to feed, she watches. She waits.

The one who called her this time is yet another who hopes to tell her story.

Like the others, his death and the rumors of her life will wield more power over many minds. His death will tell her story more than his art.

She is legend.

She is demigod.

She is Mania.

Unlike the others, she senses something familiar about him.

She feels tied to him in some old, forgotten way.

Rather than try to remember, she watches him and the woman, their bodies entwined in passion she hasn't known in ages. She feels a terrible longing, a hollowness that seems to have expanded in the time she's spent sleeping.

She longs for the worship.

For the love.

Four

Ward worked on his knees. Large sheets of paper were strewn across the hardwood floor of his living room, covered in his sketches. He preferred to storyboard himself. He had studied art in college and had almost earned enough credits to double major. Film was his first love, his vocation, but drawing was, for him, a therapeutic release. Storyboarding while Jay and Chavez shopped the script to investors helped clear his mind for production.

In the case of *The Mouth of Hell*, he had done several drawings to deal with the emotional fallout after filming wrapped on that project. He spent nights awake, on his knees in a bare apartment, sketching out the images that haunted his thoughts: The monsters from that film with their all too human faces, his father always in and out the door, the belt cinched around his mother's neck.

Now, he worked on drawing the introductory scene of *Mania*'s lead character, the unnamed actress. He had made several attempts already, but couldn't seem to get her right. While storyboards typically didn't need to be perfect, this particular drawing did need to be. He wanted to show the image to Rachel so Rachel could best understand her character's motivation. He believed that in this case, seeing the character would do more for any actress than him trying to explain, because the unnamed actress was too complex for words.

He stopped drawing and pulled his head back. The eyes were wrong. They didn't show enough. He erased.

He tried again and again.

Rachel came out of the bedroom.

"Jesus, Bill. When did you wake up?"

He blinked, stuffing down a flare of anger. "Three, I guess. What time is it now?"

They both checked the clock. Ten in the morning. He put the pencil down and shook his hand, discovering the ache for the first time.

Rachel knelt beside him. "How are they coming?"

"Good, I suppose."

She pointed at the drawing of the unnamed actress. "She's pretty. Is that how you see me? As a dashing blond American woman?"

She laughed and gave his neck a little nibble.

He pulled away. "I don't want her to just be pretty. She needs to be ... something more."

"Don't worry. I read the script. I'll make your dreams come true."

Ward stood up. "Christ, will you stop making jokes?"

She stood up too.

"Look, this story, it's important to me. I need it to be perfect."

She took a breath before she spoke. "I don't recall when I became your enemy in this. I'm your star, remember?"

He nodded, the tension releasing him the longer he stared into his lover's eyes. "You're right. I'm sorry. It's just, with this being my first film in five years and ... well, forget it. It doesn't matter."

She took his hands. "It does matter. That's why I'm here to support you."

Before he could say another word, his phone rang. He crossed the room to the end table where he had left it and answered it.

"Hol-ee shit!" Chavez said over the line. "You won't believe what just happened."

"We're funded."

In the living room, Rachel did a little twirl.

"And then some, man." Chavez laughed. "Motherfucker came to us."

"Really?"

"Yeah, not sure what sort of business he was in, but he was stacked. Dude wrote us a massive check and told us it was very important that we made this film."

"Huh. And you've never seen him before?"

Rachel's brow creased, and she mouthed the word *what*.

"Hey, who cares, right?" Chavez said.

"Yeah, I guess you're right." Ward laughed away his curiosity. "Well, shit. We're making a movie."

Five

Ward came out of his office with a stack of DVDs he had pulled from his shelf. Since the story of *Mania* was a tale of a woman in trouble, he thought Polanski's *Repulsion*, Lynch's *Inland Empire*, and Zulawski's *Possession* were ideal choices to help him prepare for the coming shoot. He held them out to Jay, who sat on the couch. They had just smoked a bowl, and Ward was starting to feel the effects.

"So what do you think?" Ward asked. "What should we watch first?"

"Definitely *Possession*." Jay took his flask from the breast pocket of his denim jacket and sipped.

"I can get you a glass for that. Some ice. A coaster. That way you don't look like such a degenerate."

Jay shrugged. "Want a hit?"

"I'll be fine."

Ward crossed the floor to the DVD player and put *Possession* into the slot. As it started up, Jay giggled.

"What?"

"Should just fast-forward to the octopus-demon on lady sex scene." Another sip. His giggle became a cackle, less controlled. "Or the miscarriage in the subway."

"You really are a strange fucker, aren't you?"

"Yup, and you hired me."

Ward had known Jay's twisted sense of humor from the first time they met. It had been two years ago, at a screening of *Atrophy* in a small theater outside of Philadelphia, where Ward had been invited to introduce the film and do a Q & A afterwards to an audience of less than fifty. All of them dressed in black and wore shirts with logos from 80s slasher films printed on them. Several of them smelled like sweat and cold cuts.

Jay had been the only one in the audience to ask intelligent questions and seemed to really understand the psychological horrors lurking beneath the lurid gore effects. While Ward was not shy in his depiction of graphic violence, his goal had always been for it to mean something, to be earned, to evoke as well as gross out. He always enjoyed finding a fan who appreciated the deeper themes in his work. Ward and Jay had met up outside of the theater afterwards and had a long conversation about Korean horror and David Cronenberg.

Where Chavez was a business partner more than anything, Ward and Jay shared a more personal connection. Aside from Rachel, who was out doing press for her newest film, Ward enjoyed spending time with Jay more than anyone else. When Jay helped Ward find his newest project, he treasured their relationship even more.

Now they sat in silence as the film started. The familiar progression of Sam Neill and Isabelle Adjani's relationship into manic, mutually destructive paranoia captivated Ward no less than it did every other time he had watched the landmark film. He'd seen it more times than he could count. He'd read every analysis of it he could find. Seeing it had been pivotal in his decision to go into making movies. He knew the film from beginning to end.

That was why in the scene where Sam Neill's character meets his child's teacher, an alternate version of his wife, Ward knew something was wrong. Instead of retaining Adjani's dark, soft hair, she appeared with dirty blond hair falling across her shoulders in wet tangles. Her skin had gone several shades paler, her eyes recessed into dark shadows.

A crawling tension began in Ward's toes and inched its way up his body, making him seize. Ward tried to say something to see if Jay noticed the change too, but only a dry croak came out. The woman on the screen turned toward Ward and smiled, showing all her teeth.

Ward cleared his throat, said, "Jay."

"Yeah, man?" His tone was nonchalant, and Ward knew right away that Jay wasn't seeing what he was seeing.

Ward glanced at his friend, then back at the screen. The regular sequence of events had resumed. The unnamed actress was gone. Isabelle Adjani was herself. The tension eased. His breath returned. *I must be really high.*

"Yo, earth to William." Jay's voice pierced through the remaining veil of Ward's reverie.

Ward shook his head. "Sorry, I just ... forget it."

Jay kept his eyes on Ward, then dug the flask back out of his jacket and held it out. This time, Ward took it.

Six

Onlookers and journalists crowded the outside of the Starland Theater, all of them wanting to get an insider look at the cast of *Black Reckoning*, particularly Dalton Carver. Cameras flashed and people talked, creating a swirling chaos of light and sound. The venue had been completely renovated a decade ago from an abandoned warehouse by a genre fan who had money to throw at pet projects. Now, all the horror premieres happened here, but the Dalton-Carver-starring *Black Reckoning* was the venue's biggest event to date.

Rachel worked her magic as they walked through the crowd. Her smile and charms came naturally, while it took effort for him to be as cordial. Crowds posed difficulties for Ward outside of a controlled environment, like the set of one of his films or an event he was hosting. Rachel tugged on his arm, and he bent down to meet her.

"You're squeezing my hand."

"Sorry."

He didn't know how Rachel held together so well. This was the closest thing to a red carpet premiere for her, and he expected her to be more nervous. The short films she had written, directed, and starred in had made her an underground darling, but as she smiled, waved, and shook hands, she fit in just fine with this considerably larger crowd.

"This is really great," he said. "I'm proud of you."

"I couldn't have done it without you, and you know that."

He kissed her, not caring that photos of their public display of affection would end up all over the internet tomorrow. They broke apart and moved forward. A dark-haired woman wearing a shiny silver dress intercepted them on the way to the entrance.

"Rachel Katayama, I'm Kelly Cain with Horror Buzz, could I have a word?"

"Sure," Rachel said. She looked to the side and giggled, her bewilderment bringing out a childlike shyness that Ward found adorable.

"How does it feel going from a cult actress to having a role with an actor of Dalton Carver's caliber?"

Ward gritted his teeth at the mention of her costar's name.

"Oh my God! Dalton Carver? Like how did this poor little indie actress hold her own?"

Ward laughed at Rachel's sarcasm. Kelly kept a straight face.

"Do you see yourself doing more mainstream films?"

"Nope, I hate big paychecks."

"What is the scariest part in *Black Reckoning*?"

"I thought this was a spoiler-free interview."

Kelly forced a laugh and turned her attention to Ward.

"William Ward, what are you up to these days?"

"I'm working on a film that people have died trying to make."

Kelly put on a saccharine smile and said, "I can't wait to see it."

Upon entering the theater, a man wearing all black ushered them to their seats.

"I wonder if she meant it," Ward said.

"What?" Rachel asked.

"She said she couldn't wait to see what I do next."

Rachel sat down and took his hand again. "Come on, you're not that obscure."

Dalton leaned forward and grinned.

"Hey, Rachel," he said.

"Dalton, hi!"

Dalton reached over and hugged Rachel. He looked at Ward, cordial, but his grin had diminished.

"Hey, Bill." He stuck out his hand. "Glad you could make it."

"Wouldn't miss it for the world," Ward said and shook Dalton's hand.

"Hey," Dalton said to the usher. "Can you get someone to bring us some drinks?"

"Sure thing, Mr. Carver," the usher said as his face turned red, then walked away with a spring in his step, checking over his shoulder a few times before finally disappearing.

Someone took their order and had their drinks out within minutes. Ward sipped his bourbon and grimaced as it went down.

"Good shit," he said and raised the glass.

"I'd raise hell for you if it wasn't," Dalton said and raised his own glass.

Ward pressed his lips together in a half-hearted attempt at a smile. He wasn't thrilled with being seated near Dalton Carver. His cockiness showed through in every mannerism. A notorious womanizer, the stories of his exploits filled the pages of tabloids and made up most of the content in all the "who's screwing who in Hollywood" blogs.

The theater darkened.

"All right, here we go," Dalton hollered.

Rachel laughed, and Ward felt a pang of jealousy.

The title card came up as charcoal drawn on gray stone. Grain had been added digitally to imitate the aesthetic of a 1970s exploitation flick, but Ward could sense the shine of a blockbuster between the grit. Dalton's name came up first.

"They paid me so fucking much to be in this piece of shit," Dalton said.

"So much for artistic integrity," Ward mumbled. Rachel flashed him a look of disapproval.

Dalton let the comment roll off his back. "Artistic integrity doesn't always pay the bills, my man."

"It does if your bills don't include eight cars and a starter castle."

"What can I say? I like nice things."

Rachel frowned and shook her head. Ward turned his attention back to the screen.

"Fair enough," Ward said as the opening death scene stained the screen red.

●●●

"What were you thinking?" Rachel said to Ward after a long, silent ride back to their apartment. He shut the front door and shrugged. "Clearly, you weren't thinking of me at all."

Ward crossed the living room to the bureau and poured himself a glass of bourbon.

"Are you trying to ruin things for me?"

"Oh, come on."

"No, Bill, I'm serious." She joined him by the bureau and poured herself a glass too. "At the premiere of my breakout movie, you insult my costar?"

"It didn't seem to bother him much."

"You could stand to be as thick-skinned."

"What the hell is that supposed to mean?"

She took a gulp of bourbon and didn't grimace or flinch. "Nothing. That was a mean thing for me to say."

She stared at him. The dim light of the apartment cast shadows across her face, but didn't hide the hurt in her eyes.

"I don't get you sometimes, Bill."

He raised his hand and let it drop to his side just as quickly.

She put down her glass. "I'm going to bed."

"I'm going to stay up for a little if you don't mind."

"Yeah, fine. Do whatever you need to do."

He held her stare for another minute. He kissed her on the lips, but lightly, impersonally.

"Good night."

"Yeah," she said. "Good night."

● ● ●

The television was a portal through which Ward escaped his world. Not in the false realities of survival programs or the sub-urban psychodramas of talk show hosts. But in film. In that way, he was his father's son. He couldn't remember a time when movies didn't consume his world. His father had been so involved in film that he had never been around, a scarcity that increased after his mother had gotten sick. When his father died, Ward wondered why he had even gone to the funeral. It had felt like attending the burial of a total stranger.

Tonight, drunkenness slowed down the world, blurred the lines, and made it easier to escape. The images on the television, made of fever dream colors and textures that only reminded him of death, became more and more vivid as he fell in and out of sleep.

From outside the blurred lines, she came. Her blond hair barely distinguishable from her pale skin. Her eyes burning silver lights, cutting through his field of vision with intense, eerie light. She walked in front of him, blocking the television from view. Her white dress clung to her pointed breasts and the angles of her hips.

He stared up at her pale silhouette, and she stared down at him. The woman's presence elicited a chill in the room's atmosphere. As if she exhaled winter. She touched his face with the icy fingertips of her skeletal hand, chilling him to his core, frosting his bones. Cold electricity coursed through his body, pleasant and terrible all at once. Ward thought this was what dying felt like.

●●●

He woke with a jolt on his couch. The television was still on, playing a spot for *Black Reckoning*. Some asshole was calling it the most terrifying movie of the year. It would have pissed him off more if the remnants of his dream didn't still have him spooked. Goosebumps textured his arms and legs. He could hear his heart pounding between his temples.

Ward's hands were shaking. On the table beside him were two empty glasses. He shut off the television and listened for anything out of the ordinary. The room was silent. Nothing seemed out of place. The front door was locked, the light was on the setting he had left it, and the door to his and Rachel's bedroom was closed. He couldn't explain the unseasonable chill in the air, though.

Seven

Rachel sat still as Alison Weaver applied her makeup. Alison had worked on Ward's previous films, part of a core group of crewmembers who worked with him on everything.

The weeks of pre-production had consisted of casting, assembling the crew, and securing locations. Tension had simmered between Ward and Rachel since the premiere of *Black Reckoning*. She attributed this to the absence of Dalton Carver in their lives. While she disliked that peace had come about by not confronting the issues, she was glad to have the peace at all. Even more so, it pleased her to be working again with Ward and his loyal crew.

Allison put down the makeup brush and stepped away.

"You look hot," she said. She giggled. "I mean, if I do say so myself! Have a looksee."

Rachel turned in the chair to face the mirror.

And she screamed.

The face looking back at her was not her own. The skin had taken on the grayish pallor of death. One eye was clouded over, the other gone altogether, replaced by a cavernous red hole. Her hair was now a tangled mess, caked with blood and dirt.

Rachel threw herself from the stool and backed across the room, nearly knocking Alison down.

"What? What is it?" Alison asked.

Rachel stared at her for a frantic moment, unsure of how Alison could have missed what she had seen. She looked back at the mirror.

She was herself again. A little dolled-up with hair dyed platinum blond, but herself. She looked from the mirror to Alison. Alison's eyes stared wide. Her lips moved as if trying to find words. People knew Rachel for the way she carried herself with poise. Freaking out was not in her nature.

"I'm okay, I just ..." Rachel tried to think of how she could possibly finish that sentence. She got up. "I just need to get out of here for a few minutes."

"You sure you're good?"

Someone knocked on the dressing room door, and both girls jumped.

"What's going on in there?" Jay's voice.

Rachel took a breath. "We're fine. We just saw a spider. Crisis averted."

Alison frowned at her.

"Okay," Jay said and walked away.

"A spider, Rachel?"

"Just forget it." She looked in the mirror again and smiled upon seeing herself in character, not rotting. "You did a great job, Alison, as usual."

She gave the artist a hug and left the dressing room.

Inside the mirror, someone watched.

●●●

Ward stared through the camera at Rachel as she wandered through the crowd of extras, lost and scared. The actress's arrival in Hollywood after running away from home. Rachel was nailing it, the frantic glances around, the conflicting emotions of wonder and fear playing in her features.

He stepped back as she drew closer, keeping the camera focused on her face and neck. His D.P., Julian, kept pace with her and filmed her from the side. Ward hoped Julian's shot would also capture Rachel's reflection in the glass wall of the building. Of course it would. He trusted Julian's eye.

He stopped backing up and let Rachel come face to face with his camera before yelling, "Cut."

He wanted to hug her, but refrained. On set, he tried to keep the public displays of affection to a minimum. He didn't want to give the impression he was treating anyone differently. He settled on a smile and said, "Nice job."

She smiled back, but the haunted expression still held her eyes, as if she hadn't broken character.

"You okay?"

She hesitated, then nodded. "Yeah, everything's fine."

He didn't believe her. He fought the urge to pull her aside and ask what was wrong. Julian came walking up.

"Good shit from my angle. What's next?"

"Where's my script?" Ward asked.

Jay trotted over, holding the pages in his hands. Rachel sat down as the three men went over Ward's notes. Julian stared past Ward at her.

"You sure you're all right?" he asked. "Fuckin' look like ..."

She tried to smile. "I'm fine."

"She's fine," Ward said. "Our next scene is number twenty-five. Let's get it set up."

Rachel remained seated as the crew readied the scene. Without Julian finishing the sentence, she knew he'd been about to say, *Fuckin' look like you've seen a ghost.*

Eight

Ward had wanted to make movies since he was six years old and discovered that making movies could be a job. First, he had wanted to impress his father. As his father's fame grew and he spent less time being a father, Ward decided to make films to spite the old man. If Stephen Ward was Spielberg, William Ward would be von Trier. Deodato. Lenzi. Instead of flights of fancy about the so-called goodness of the human spirit, he would tell stories about the way things really were. Expose the ugliness.

Now, with his father in the ground for the past five years, Ward saw himself as less angry, but still compelled to raw honesty. He detected the unrestrained approach to pain that had become his trademark in the footage, but also something bigger, a cinematic grandiosity that he associated with his father's films. He shifted in his seat, uncomfortable with the realization.

Rachel massaged his shoulders from behind.

"It looks good," she said.

"You look good."

She grunted. "I never get used to watching myself."

"Must've been hard when you were editing and directing all your own stuff."

"You have no idea. Guess I'm lucky you were the only one crazy enough to watch my films." She leaned down and kissed his forehead.

She was being humble. A lot of people liked the short films she had made in Japan. Fans and people in the industry had called her the crowned princess of cult horror. But now that Hollywood knew her, people saw her as just another hard-working B-movie actress. Maybe he hadn't really done Rachel any favors.

"So, what was wrong earlier?" he asked. "And don't say 'nothing,' I know you better than that."

She stopped massaging his shoulders and withdrew her hands.

Ward turned his office chair around. "Rachel?"

She blinked and peered down at him as if noticing him in the room with her for the first time. "I just … her story … it's so sad."

Ward rose and folded his arms around her, an embrace that she returned. A tear slid down her cheek. The story was sad. The actress had been used by everyone around her and never had a firm grasp on how to make the best of her situation. She had died alone and betrayed, like she herself had been cursed.

● ● ●

Ward dreamed of his father's grave, a place he hadn't visited since the funeral. A blue pool of sky encased the earth below. No wind blew against his skin. No threat of rain ached in his bones. The temperate day could have either been mid-spring or early summer.

Ward ran his finger along the clear, detailed etching in the marble headstone, the letters of his father's name, the hammer-and-serpent seal of Stephen Ward's production company, the dates of birth and death.

Unsure now if dreaming or awake, Ward bowed before the headstone. He didn't pray–he almost never did—but he let himself be silent. A distant part of him knew that he had just completed the first day of shooting *Mania*. Unsure if that mattered, he tried to let the moment speak to him.

The headstone reflected the bright glare from the sun. The brilliance burned his eyes, but he couldn't turn away. His gaze drew further into the light until his vision whited out. Nothing existed now except for Ward's consciousness, disembodied in the paleness that surrounded it.

Darker spots, like sunspots, morphed into bubbling, swirling forms and danced in the light, solidifying and taking shape. The puzzle pieces collected around a pulsing black heart.

The shape grew into a version of Stephen Ward, his face the quality of plastic sizzling in a bonfire. It oozed, pieces peeling off in charred, fleshy clumps.

The image spoke in words Ward couldn't understand, but he recognized his father's condescending tone. A scream welled up inside of Ward, starting in his guts and catching in his throat. He thought he would choke on the unspoken cry.

The vision burned before his eyes, opening into his living room. Dalton had Rachel bent over the arm of the microfiber sofa. She screamed in both pleasure and pain as Dalton drilled into her from behind. The actor looked up from Rachel's slim but shapely ass and grinned at Ward.

Dalton never spoke, but Ward heard the words implied by the grin just the same.

See this? I'm nailing your girl, and there's not shit you can do about it. I bet you'd like to hit me, wouldn't you? Knock this smug look right off my face. But it ain't happening.

Ward tried to step forward to do just that, but his legs locked into place.

The unreleased scream still sat as a hard lump in his throat, blocking his airway.

He tried to close his eyes against the offending image, but even they defied him. They forced him to see his lover have a hissing, teeth-gritting orgasm with another man. Her fingernails dug deep grooves into the arm of the sofa, and a scream tore from her lungs.

Inside his mind, Ward willed himself to wake. He couldn't take any more of this.

"Yeah, bitch," Dalton said. "Fuck yeah."

"Oh God, yeah," Rachel said, moaning like a crazed animal.

No.

I'm dreaming.

This can't be happening.

Can it? Can Rachel really be doing this to me?

She cried out. Dalton continued to groan his own pleasure. All the while, Ward's scream remained suppressed. He thought he really would choke on it, even wished he would. Once dead, he would have no dreams. No memories. Nothing.

Nothing.

● ● ●

Upon waking, he remembered the time his grandmother had pulled him out of the pool. Ward had been no more than two years old.

Now he lay in bed, a pale hand clutching his. The unnamed actress stood above him, her blond hair hanging down like curtains beside the window of her face. She smiled at him, her skin glowing, fluorescent.

"How did you …?"

And in a blink, she was gone. Ward lay alone in his bedroom, staring up at the flat ceiling. Instead of expelling the scream lodged in his throat, he gasped for air and glanced around. The air held a subtle chill. The door stood open a crack. Beyond it, daylight.

● ● ●

Red tulips sat in a skinny variegated vase. Ward walked over and ran his fingertips along their soft petals. Their fresh scent went straight to his head. He flashed a look at Rachel, who was sitting on the sectional in the next room with her iPad open in her lap.

"Where'd these come from?" Ward asked, but had a feeling he knew.

Rachel must have sensed his apprehension, because she hesitated before she answered. Ward walked over to the sofa and sat down beside her.

"Dalton's sending you flowers now?"

Rachel smiled and looked up from the website she was reading. "*Black Reckoning* was nominated for a Chainsaw Award. He sent them to say 'congrats.' That's all."

"If you say so."

His arm encircled her bare shoulders and massaged the side of her arm. She cooed in response to his touch, kissed him on the nose. Their eyes met, and he tried to stare deeper inside her.

The presence of the tulips after such a terrible dream made for an uncomfortable coincidence. He wanted to let go and trust her, to resolve that Dalton was slime and she would never go for someone like that. Logic dictated this, but a darker part of him insisted he worry. This inner darkness had been there a long time, and in some of Ward's more turbulent years, he had allowed it to flourish, stretching its corrupt influence into every other aspect of his personality. *Atrophy* had been born out of this darkness.

Rachel put her iPad aside and hopped into Ward's lap, clearing his thoughts. She bit him gently on the neck, sending tingling sensations across his flesh.

"I haven't even had my coffee yet," he said.

"This is better than coffee," she said and reached down to fumble with his pajama pants.

No arguments there. He ran his hand under her black tank top, pressing his fingers against her smooth skin. Its warmth brought his desires to full attention. He put his lips to her throat and kissed aggressively, drawing gasps of pleasure out of her.

As he kissed, she worked him with her hands. Ward shut his eyes, carried away by pleasure. She pulled her panties aside.

"Are you ready?" she asked.

"God, yes."

Rachel slid down onto him, and he dug his nails into the soft flesh beneath her rib cage. Rachel cried out, but continued uninhibited, finding her rhythm as she rode him. She arched her back, pressing his face between her small breasts. He licked one nipple, then the other. Her gyrations intensified.

Ward laid her down on the cushions and caught the tulips in his line of sight. Dalton's tulips. Ward collapsed into her arms and closed his eyes. In the darkness, he recalled the dream: the image of Dalton slamming into Rachel on the very same couch.

Tension built inside him as he thrust into Rachel. He tried to fuck away the troubling image, but it grew clearer instead, so vivid he could see the beads of sweat on Dalton's toned skin.

Yeah, bitch. Dalton's voice as clear as if he was standing in the room with them.

With a grunt, Ward pulled out and turned Rachel onto her belly, bracing her against the arm of the sectional. He entered her from behind. She yelped in surprise, but not without pleasure. Ward opened his eyes to view their perfect union between her ass cheeks, then traced the length of her body with his fingertips. Her skirt had come up around her midsection, and her hair hung around her face. Her hands kneaded the fabric of the sofa.

Ward's gaze wandered to the tulips, and he thrust harder into her. The flowers held his sight, becoming his sole focus. Like a bull, he only saw red. He increased speed and intensity. Her screams and the color red only fueled him. His senses exploded around him, within him.

He clasped his hands over hers and pinned them to the couch. With the newfound leverage, he went even deeper, causing her screams to become cries of pain. She was saying something too, but he couldn't hear her. The taunting image had him hypnotized.

"Goddamn it, Bill! You're hurting me!"

He ignored her.

"Bill, stop it!"

He grabbed a handful of her hair and pulled.

"What the hell is wrong with you, damn it!"

He came, a high-voltage surge of energy expelling from his body, and with a final cry, he collapsed on top of her

"What the fuck?" Rachel rolled out from under him and stood up, eyeing him with a fury he had never before witnessed from her. "Didn't you fucking hear me?"

Ward shook his head. He knew he had lost control, like something else had commandeered his body, driven by the troubling images. A violent pounding filled his head. His breath zipped in and out of his mouth. What scared him most was that he had heard her protests but couldn't stop hurting her.

"Fuck." Rachel stomped down the hallway to the bathroom and slammed the door behind her.

Ward dropped his head in his hands and stared at his bare feet sinking into the carpet. He took stock of his thoughts, found them rational, his own. He told himself the flowers had triggered the unpleasant memory of the dream, setting his anger to a boil. Combined with the passion of the moment, his emotions had taken control. Knowing this did little to improve how he felt.

He looked at the tulips, sitting in the vase, mocking him.

Nine

Day two of the shoot. Jay pulled Ward aside during lunch break.

The set was an old motel on the outskirts of the city, and Chavez had arranged for a catering company owned by his aunt to serve food in the lobby. Ward had chosen the location because the script had named it as the setting for this scene. Using it gave a sense of authenticity.

Ward followed Jay out of the lobby and across the drop-off lane to the designated smoking area. Jay pulled out his flask and offered Ward a sip. Ward held up his hand and shook his head. After Jay finished sipping, Ward asked, "What's up?"

"You tell me."

Ward fought the urge to look away. "What are you talking about?"

"Come on."

"Come on, what? Nothing's going on."

"Don't lie to me, bro."

Ward scrunched leaves of the bush behind him between his fingers. He thought not of the events that had transpired that morning, but of the unnamed actress appearing in the Zulawski film and his dreams.

Jay raised an eyebrow. "Lose the hundred-yard stare. Talk to me."

Ward tore the leaf off of a twig and let it fall behind him.

"I don't know, Jay. I think I'm losing my mind."

"Meaning?"

"Well, remember that day we watched that Zulawski film?"

"Always remember watching Zulawski."

Jay laughed. Ward didn't.

"Seriously, though, what happened?"

"I saw something in the film. Something that wasn't there before."

"Dude, high as we were? Surprised you didn't see Jesus riding a pink tapir." Jay's features hardened. "Not what you saw, was it?"

Ward sighed. "Sorry, I'm not in much of a laughing mood."

"Really freaked you out, huh? Well, like I said, we were really high. Different stuff than the usual batch I get too, I think. What you see anyway?"

"Marielle." Ward mumbled it, barely wanting to admit something so strange.

"Who?"

"The unnamed actress. Guess she has a name now."

"The chick from our script?"

"Yeah."

"Damn. Think we're cursed?"

Ward considered this. Jay's eyes widened at the delayed response.

"Don't be ridiculous," Ward said.

"Don't sound so convinced. See anything else?"

"Have you seen anything?"

Jay shrugged. "Not at all."

"Have you been feeling off or anything?"

"No, but get it if you are. You're working again. Not just on the distro side, but directing again. Gotta be a load of stress after being away so long."

Yes, Ward thought. *That's all it is. Stress.*

"Come on, what's the other option? Haunted script? Vengeful ghost?" Jay hooked his hands into claws and rolled his eyes into the back of his head. He moaned like a zombie.

"Yeah, I guess you're right," Ward said.

Logic took hold. Of course Jay was right. The image on the film had been drug-related. The dreams were just dreams. Ward owed Rachel an apology.

Jay clapped him on the shoulder. "Knew I could cheer you up. You are cheered up, right?"

"As good as I'm gonna get."

"Hey, come on. We're making a movie. How fucking cool is that?"

Ward grinned. He had to commend Jay's enthusiasm. It almost made Ward forget his own unease.

"So how you come up with the name? Marielle?" Jay asked.

"I'm not sure. Just came to me, I guess."

Ward thought he had heard it in his dreams.

After finishing his lunch, Julian stepped outside to smoke. He crossed paths with Ward and Jay and nodded at them. He wondered for a brief moment what that may have been about and let it drift from his thoughts.

He reached the smoking area and lit a cigarette. A nasty habit he had picked up from his older brother when they had been at San Diego State together. He planned to quit one day, but didn't think about it too often.

As he stood and smoked, a red car parked beside him caught his eye. He turned to examine it. A 1963 Mercury Comet. Other than film, Julian's other passion was cars. The fully restored hot rod captured his attention, leaving the cigarette to burn unsmoked in his hand. Every detail flawless, its recent wax glistened in the sun.

He rounded the front, stopping to examine the headlights and chrome grill. When he raised his head to look at the windshield, he saw her standing behind him.

Aside from the fact that she was holding her guts in her hands, Julian found her beautiful. A blond in a white dress, the kind of girl who would look great behind the wheel of a classic Mercury Comet. Her reflection smiled at him.

He blinked, and she was still there, chunks of torn intestine dripping from between her fingers and spattering the pavement.

"Oh fuck."

Her grin spread. She whispered his name. Though her reflection showed her to be at least ten feet behind him, he heard it as if her lips pressed against his ear.

She uncoiled a length of intestine, held it out like a hose, then brought it to her lips. Her tongue slipped out, and she ran it along the organ's length, keeping a fuck-me stare locked on Julian the entire time. She slid the intestine into her mouth and sucked on its end. Blood smeared her mouth like badly applied lipstick.

Julian's mouth opened and closed, unable to speak, to scream. His spit drained from his palate. His blood throbbed—in his head, in his chest, in his cock. Scared, but inexplicably aroused, he couldn't take his eyes off of her.

She ran the length of intestine down her body, smearing her dress with blood and shit. With her other hand, she lifted its hem, showed her bald pussy, and slid the ropey organ inside.

His fingers trembled, then sizzled as heat enveloped them.

"Fuck, shit, goddamn it!"

His cigarette had burned down to the filter, leaving a red mark on his index and middle fingers. His heart beat like marching feet on his chest. He checked the wound, spun to face the parking lot, and wiped at his eyes.

The woman was gone.

Maybe Rachel pulling a prank, he thought. *No, no fucking way.*

All but his eyes froze as he scanned his surroundings. He couldn't see the woman anywhere. She had just vanished.

Nothing just goddamn disappears. Definitely not disemboweled fucking women. She had to have gone somewhere. He couldn't remember the last time he had felt so anxious, the last time his thoughts had moved so erratically. He prided himself on his ability to control his emotions, but that control had gone and so had his pride.

"Hey, Julian," said a voice from the motel. "You ready?"

Jay stood just outside the lobby.

"Yeah," he said, trying to sound as collected as possible. He couldn't wipe the image of the woman from his mind. He shook his head. "Yeah ... fuck no."

He turned and ran, ignoring all sense of professionalism, ignoring Jay's calls. All the while, he saw her over and over, fucking herself with a length of intestine.

Ten

Despite the constant pressures of diminishing daylight, Julian up and quitting, and the tension between Ward and Rachel, the rest of the day went smoothly. And no one else saw a ghost.

Jay caught up with Ward before leaving the set.

"Well, how you feeling?"

"A little better," Ward said. Not a total lie. Finishing a day of shooting always relieved stress. "Bummed about Julian, though."

"Yeah. Don't know what that's all about. Won't answer any of my calls."

"Mine either."

"Right, well, need anything, call."

Ward nodded. Jay was a good kid.

Rachel met him by his car, and they drove home.

"Rachel, I'm sorry."

She looked out the window, saying nothing. The setting sun filled the sky with fiery streaks. Ward waited another few seconds.

"Rachel ..."

"Does the fact that Dalton sent me flowers really bother you?"

Ward sighed. "No. It did, but fuck it. They're just flowers, right?"

"Of course." Another long stretch of silence passed between them. She opened her mouth, then closed it. Sighed. "You know I'd never do anything to hurt you, right?"

He considered her words. Did he know that for sure? Did he know anything for sure?

Don't be stupid. She loves you. She's telling you the truth.

The ritualized thoughts sounded like a mantra meant to reassure him of something when he feared the opposite was true. He didn't know where these feelings came from; he'd never known himself to be overly jealous. He thought of his blind rage earlier that morning. He feared his behavior had changed something irreparably, not just between him and Rachel, but in some other deeper way he had yet to understand.

"I'm really sorry, Rachel," he said again, because, really, there was nothing else he could say.

"Just don't let it happen again. I mean it."

Her words stung like daggers, but he knew he deserved it.

"I won't. I love you, Rachel."

"I love you too," she said.

But still, things had shifted in some way. Despite his and Rachel's reconciliation, they hadn't changed back.

Eleven

Tara stared at Jay across the table in the diner, either entranced by what he had to say or excellent at faking it. He couldn't figure out which, but didn't care either way.

After the first few days of shooting, he needed a night out with a nice girl. Enter Tara: not an aspiring actress, no script in her back pocket. Rare qualities in this town. He had been drawn to her Tinder profile immediately. It also helped that she was smoking hot.

"So, how'd you find it?"

"I first heard of *Mania* at a convention in the area. I found a lot more info on a website called Hollywood Inferno, an archive of allegedly true ghost stories that took place here. I thought it was crazy that people who'd tried filming the script either died or lost their shit." He gave a dry laugh. "I've always been into fucked up ghost stories and urban legends, so I looked into it, asked around on forums, and heard the only copy of the screenplay belonged to some eccentric old guy who lives just outside Hollywood. We wrote him a check, and here we are."

"Do you believe the stories?"

"I believe all of the bad shit happened. I don't believe it's because of a curse, if that's what you mean."

"That's what I mean. Do you believe in ghosts at all?"

He thought about this. "My instinct is to say no, but truthfully, I can't give you a definite answer."

"Smart boy." She reached out and touched his hand. "You ready to blow this joint?"

"I think you read my mind."

She squeezed his hand. "I'm going to use the little girls' room first."

"I'll pay the bill."

She smiled at him as she got up. "You don't have to do that."

"Can I anyway?"

"I guess I won't stop you." She rolled her eyes, then surprised him by planting a kiss on his cheek. "Thanks for dinner."

●●●

Tara sifted through her enormous body bag of a purse until she found the right shade of lipstick. The diner's bathroom was poorly lit, and the bulb above the sink flickered. She would have to work fast if she wanted to put on the burgundy wine lipstick straight.

As she steadied her hand, she became aware of a faint buzz that accompanied the flicker of the bulb. It mildly annoyed her. How could a place of business let their facilities fall into such deterioration? In addition to the blinking bulb, a piss smell hung in the air, overpowering a small hint of cleaner. A ball of toilet paper sat crumpled in one corner.

So gross. She couldn't get out of there soon enough. Even the food had been unimpressive. Dry pork chops served with mashed potatoes that had come from a box and canned corn. She had already made up her mind that she wouldn't be calling Jay again, or returning his calls. He was lucky he was cute. That was all that kept her from parting ways with him as soon as she left the restroom. Who takes a girl to a dump like this?

He was cute, though. At least *make-out with in the parking lot* material. Whether or not he was *fuck me in the back seat of a car* material depended on how he kissed. She really needed to meet better guys, she thought. She had expected better from Hollywood, but didn't know why.

She finished applying her lipstick. Even in the dim light, she decided she looked great. Dark eyes and full lips stood out like wondrous landmarks on a face lit with youthful glow. She was twenty-three and had plenty of time to meet guys. For now, she could at least have fun with bad boys and dipshits. She pursed her lips together and made to kiss her reflection when the lights went out.

This time they didn't flicker back on.

"Fucking great."

She waited another five seconds. The darkness remained. Now she would have to feel around for the exit and hope she didn't step in a puddle of urine. It shouldn't be too hard.

Still, there was something about the dark. No matter how old she was, how much of a grownup she considered herself to be, being utterly blinded and alone in its embrace set her pulse to a nervous rhythm. She hated to admit it, but the dark still scared her. She could step in something gross. She could run into something and hurt herself. Or, worst of all, she could find she wasn't completely alone.

Stop it! Just turn around, walk to the exit. It's just a few paces, ten at the most. And you can see light peeking through the crack at the bottom of the door. Just head toward—

The light flicked back on and brought her out of her thoughts. In the mirror, she saw the other woman. *Woman* was too nice of a description.

The face was vaguely feminine, but she could only tell from the bone structure. The skin hung in gray flaps, like moldy paper. Hair that may have once been blond sat upon the figure's head in manic tangles caked with dirt and blood. What scared Tara the most were the eyes. Still intact though so much else of the body had decayed, they glistened like shiny silver coins around black pupils.

The way those eyes regarded Tara stirred a childhood memory of the time her cat, Hera, had cornered her parakeet, Simon. The cat's eyes had gone wide, black pupils zeroed in on its prey. Simon's wings had been clipped, and he couldn't get away before Hera tore him into bloody, feathery pieces.

The thing in the mirror's eyes shone like a predator sizing up its prey.

Before Tara could scream, ashen arms reached out and took fistfuls of her hair. Her full burgundy lips met the pus-dripping, black lips of the woman in the mirror. A wart-studded tongue pushed between Tara's teeth and oozed, filling her mouth with a viscous, custardy fluid. A knobby wart brushed against Tara's tonsils, engaging her gag reflex. Vomit lurched from her guts and mixed with the thick gunk from the woman's mouth.

Tara flailed, tried to push away as she choked on rancid fluids and bitter bile. She pushed against the mirror, slapped at the woman holding her, tried to scream. The woman twisted Tara's hair, pulled her toward the mirror.

White hot pain flashed in her head as it met the filthy glass. Through blurry vision, she saw her reflection. A wound gushed between her eyes. Gray and yellow fluid poured down her chin. Her skin had gone pale gray. With the woman's lips away from hers, Tara tried to scream again.

The specter pulled her toward the mirror again. This time, her face shredded as the glass shattered. Her head sunk into the glass, into the wall. An ear tore loose, dropped in the grimy sink. The rotten lips met hers again, and this time, they didn't let go.

●●●

In the parking lot, Jay moved in for a kiss. Tara met his lips and sucked his tongue into her mouth. *Ferocious*, he thought. *Jay, my friend, you've done well tonight.*

He hoped she would be okay with a no-strings-attached arrangement. He wasn't ready to settle down. He was still young and far from ready to give up casual encounters like this one.

She pulled her lips from his. Her eyes burned with desire as she glared at him.

"So, my place or yours?" he asked. Sloppy, but the way she kissed him made him feel like his chances were good.

Her lips spread into a devious smile. "What's wrong with your car?"

A wave of giddiness rose inside him. He felt like a lap dog in a room full of legs. "Nothing at all."

He took out his keys and led her by the hand toward his Honda, feeling a sense of accomplishment. It had been a good two days of shooting, and, on top of that, he was about to score. He unlocked the car, opened the door to the back seat, and turned to smile at Tara, gesturing for her to enter.

"You first."

He nodded and complied. On his way inside, she smacked his ass and he giggled. She climbed in behind him and shut the door. Her tongue slid across her lips.

"Lie down," she said.

"Yes, ma'am."

He rested his head against the car door and put his feet up underneath her. She dropped a knee on either side of his lap, her skirt spreading out across her thighs. Her heat almost made him explode in his pants, so he bit his lip and tried to think about things that didn't turn him on, like Sean Connery's codpiece in the movie

Zardoz or his Aunt Kathy trying to squeeze all two-hundred-fifty pounds of her girth into a skimpy bathing suit.

Tara reached down and yanked his pants off without undoing the belt. His legs burned from the friction, and he winced. She smiled at his pain.

"Did I hurt you?" she asked with a pout.

God damn, she was sexy.

She crawled across his body and brought her knees down beside his head. She took a handful of her black panties and tore the garment off.

"Jesus ..."

She giggled. "Trust me, Jay, you don't want Him to be around us tonight."

Tara brought her dripping sex closer to his face, and he breathed in its perfumes. She smelled like what he imagined heaven would smell like, strawberries with a creamy finish. He brought his mouth up to meet her, and she sat down on his face.

He licked with enthusiasm, happy to earn his keep in her pussy. Anything that kept him from coming early would have been satisfactory, but this ... this was special. She had sat on his face without him asking.

She grinded harder against him. It hurt, but he reveled in it. He hooked his arms around her thighs and tried to control her rhythm. She gripped him by the forearms and tore his hands away. She pressed them against the warm window.

A putrid scent wafted from inside of her as she leaked into his mouth. He gagged and tried to shove her off, but she pressed down against him, tightened her quads. He tried to free his hands, but her strength overpowered him. The viscous fluid poured down his throat, and he choked. He tried to scream, but her vulva covered his mouth and muffled his cries.

Tendrils slithered out of her and wrapped around his head, holding it in place. If he had any vague hope that he would escape this, it died as another, much thicker, tentacle snaked down his throat.

Jay writhed in her vile embrace, the fight draining out of him every second, life force pouring out from a deep place as the creature that lived in her sex sucked with greed.

So much for not believing in curses.

Twelve

"Jay, it's me. Where the hell are you, man?" Ward hung up after leaving his third message.

Devon, Julian's replacement, sat beside Ward, holding a camera in his lap. He grimaced. "That's some shit."

"It's just not like him, man. I've known him for a few years now. He's a consummate professional."

"Apparently not."

Ward ignored the offhand comment. He tried to forget this was the second person to disappear from set in as many days. Anger stirred within him, but his rationality told him that there had to be a logical reason for this. Julian had quit. Jay probably had a good excuse for not being here too. Probably just stuck in traffic or something.

"Whatever. We'll just have to get started without him."

He picked up his script and entered the day's location: an abandoned suite in an abandoned strip mall. The long closed-down building had been a kickboxing studio in its previous life. Some towels and a few old pads sat scattered throughout the premise. A thick scent of ancient sweat mixed with dust lent the place an atmosphere of age and physical strain. Several jugs of cleaner sat against one of the walls. Though a possible fire hazard, Ward hadn't had the jugs removed. The atmosphere of the place was too perfect to upset.

Rachel came in behind them, dressed in a black vinyl skirt and a red tube top. She carried herself with poise, the haunted look long gone from her features. She'd spent the morning preparing for the scene ahead.

Ward read the words on the page: *THE ACTRESS leads RICK into the abandoned gym. She goes to kiss him, but he throws her to the ground.* Ward closed his eyes.

When he opened them, Rachel stood before him.

"Any word?"

"No. I wish I knew where the hell Jay was." He waved his hand. "Never mind me. How are you? Are you ready for this scene?"

"We're doing it early in the shoot for a reason, right?"

Ward nodded. She kissed him on the corner of his mouth and offered a smile. He didn't mind at all that she'd kissed him in front of the crew this time. Emotional exhaustion had settled over him this morning, even before Jay no-showed. He felt drained. Maybe the beginnings of a virus.

With the scene set up, Ward called action. The cameras rested on tripods, an older practice, but Ward didn't want to cut away. A scene so pivotal, so filled with pain, he had a responsibility to show everything.

He believed in pain as a doorway to rebirth. Though he'd never been a Marine, he liked their old saying: pain is just weakness leaving the body. After shooting *The Mouth of Hell* and descending into the pits of depression, he believed he emerged stronger, better. He saw this scene as a turning point in the film. An ugly experience for the character, sure, but a big step toward catharsis for the audience.

He watched the scene through his camera. Rachel led Nelson Miles, the actor portraying Rick, to the center of the room. He moved in slow, deliberate steps. His broad shoulders heaved as he looked Rachel up and down, animal hunger in his eyes. An unknown, his menacing demeanor had impressed Ward during his audition.

Rachel turned to face Nelson. She rose on her tiptoes and went in for a kiss. He returned it for a beat, grabbed her by the shoulders, and threw her to the ground. She hit the floor, and before she could get back up, he collapsed upon her. He pinned her arms with his knees and gripped her hair in his hands.

"Pretty thing," he said. "Are you scared?"

She whimpered.

"Go ahead, let it out. Show me how afraid you are."

She shook her head and tried to pull out from under him.

"Huh? That all you can give me? How about you scream for Uncle Ricky?" He shook her.

Only acting, Ward thought. *I've shot worse than this.*

Still, unease swam in the pit of his stomach as Rachel tried to pull free from Nelson's grasp, like the bigger man was hurting her. Nelson pulled back and slapped her face. The wet sound sent unpleasant tremors through Ward's body. He closed his eyes, took a breath, and opened them again. He kept the camera rolling.

"Fucking bitch, you don't get to say 'no' now. I paid for this, remember?"

She screamed, the shrill cry like a dagger in Ward's heart. *Too real*, he thought. *Something is wrong.* He rolled back his shoulders to keep the tension out of his neck.

Nelson pulled his hand back and balled it into a fist.

It's okay. The script calls for this. He won't really hit her.

But he did. The punch connected with Rachel's nose. A sound of crunching bone reverberated in the spacious room. Blood sprayed from her face.

"Cut." Ward ran out from behind his camera. "What the fuck, Nelson?"

Nelson stood as Ward approached. Ward shoved him. "You really fucking hit her, man. What the fuck is wrong with you?"

At the physical contact, Nelson's eyes hardened. He bit his lip for a split second, then relaxed his face. "What the hell are you talking about?"

"You just coldcocked her. What kind of—"

"Bill," Rachel said.

He spun around at the sound of her voice. Concern held her unbroken features. Ward looked for signs of blood on her face, her clothes, and the floor. Nothing.

"Motherfucker."

He glanced from Rachel to Nelson. The hardness had returned to Nelson's face. He stuck a meaty finger at Ward.

"You're lucky I'm a professional. Otherwise you'd wish you'd never shoved me."

Ward tried to think of a retort, but came up empty. Probably for the best. Nelson was right. He scanned the rest of the room. His crew eyed him with a mixture of concern and amusement.

He put up his hand. "Look, I'm sorry. I thought I saw you hit her. Obviously, I was mistaken. Can we just pick up the scene again?"

"That depends. You gonna start shit with me again?" Nelson said.

In his mind, Ward already saw the actors' union nightmare unfolding. He needed to make peace with Nelson later, after everyone cooled down.

"All right, everyone, I'm sorry about that. We're gonna shoot it again, from the top." He thought for a minute. "Julian. Sorry, Devon. I'll need you to operate the camera. I think I need some fresh air."

Rachel raised her eyebrows.

"I'll be fine, Rachel. Just do the scene. I'll be back once my head is clear."

The door burst open and Chavez stormed in, his white shirt drenched in sweat. He sucked in a lungful of air and leaned his considerable bulk against an old end table.

"What is it?" Ward asked.

"It's Jay, man."

Ward's earlier unease resurfaced. What little breakfast he'd eaten threatened to come back up.

"I just got off the phone with his mom." He used his forearm to wipe sweat from his face. "They found him in his car."

"What happened?" Rachel asked.

"Police ain't saying shit."

The news crushed Ward to his knees. Jay was still just a kid. Early twenties. He hadn't even moved out of his parents' basement yet, but he was so full of enthusiasm and possessed a deep affinity for film, and life. Reality set in, and physical pain accosted Ward's body.

There wouldn't be any more shooting today.

● ● ●

Rachel held the steering wheel in an iron grip. She kept it steady and centered. Anything could take that control from her, a car slamming into her, a cyclist pulling out in front of her. It wouldn't take much. Her hold on her life had a similar lack of integrity.

Ward sat in the passenger seat not saying a word as they passed buildings and cars. No emotion marked his features. That scared her more than if he had gotten angry or cried. Showing emotion at least meant that he was ready to deal with emotion. If he buried it, the feelings would fester until its poison could no longer be contained. He could have another breakdown. At least that's what his old therapist, Dr. Schuler, had said. Though five years had passed, she couldn't emotionally deal with nursing him through another dark period like that.

She had watched him take to self-harm like an adolescent. He would drink himself into psychotic trances where he would distrust everyone around him, even her. She had stuck with him because she owed him. No, she didn't just owe him; she loved him.

Rachel put her hand on Ward's knee. "Look, I'm not going to ask you if you're all right. I know you're not. I'm not going to ask you what you're thinking about either, because I'm sure I know. What I will do is tell you that I'm here if you need to talk. Because you will. It's not good to keep it inside."

"Yeah." His gaze fell to his lap. "I'm sorry about earlier. I'm not sure what came over me."

Jay's death had her so preoccupied, she had almost forgotten about that. Recalling it sent a chill through her body. Ward's anger in that moment and the previous morning reminded her of the dark days, the fallout after production on *The Mouth of Hell*. She had told him she wouldn't ask, but she would have given anything to read his mind.

Her phone rang in her purse at Ward's feet. She reached down and answered without looking at the caller ID.

"Hello?"

"Rachel, it's Dalton."

"Hey ... what's going on?"

"Oh, nothing much. We never did have that drink."

"I've been busy." He had called once, and she had ignored him. After some thought, she had decided it would be a bad idea to see him. Other than the time their paths had crossed at the premiere of *Black Reckoning* and the flowers, there had been no interaction.

"Who is it?" Ward asked.

She held up her finger and gave him a look that she hoped conveyed she would be off the phone soon.

"Anyway," Dalton said, "you'll never guess who I met today."

"I can't even begin to imagine."

"Mark Detrik."

"Who?"

"Mark Detrik. You don't know who that is? He was supposed to be in that movie you and your boyfriend are trying to make. He was cast the first time it went into production back in eighty-seven. Man, has he got some fucked up, crazy stories."

Her nerves sizzled. "Seriously, man, bad fucking timing."

"What'd I say?"

"I'll call you later." She hung up.

Ward frowned. "Who the hell was that?"

"Dalton."

"He has your number?"

"Yeah, we exchanged numbers after we wrapped. Not a big deal. It's harmless."

Ward's eyes hardened. "Is it?"

She took a breath and adjusted her hold on the steering wheel. This was too much at once. She thought about what Dalton said. Crazy stories. What sort of crazy stories? Just a few days ago, she would've written off anything pertaining to the screenplay's curse as just that: crazy stories. Now, though, between whatever she had seen in the mirror, Ward's outbursts, Julian quitting, and the death of Jay ...

Coincidences. That's all. Just get home, relax, and be there for Bill. We'll start filming again, and things will go fine.

But as she drove, she couldn't bring herself to look in the mirrors.

Thirteen

She rides with them in the car.

Wants to taste them so bad. Feel their essence drain into her.

Fueling her.

Fulfilling her.

But timing is everything.

It has to be deliberate. It has to have purpose.

Otherwise, she is no more than an animal.

Animals have no testament to their kills.

They're doing nothing more than feeding.

Her kills tell a story.

They grow the fear.

The faith.

Give her the reverence she never knew in life.

She settles in and lets the life forces from the previous night's prey stir within her. Gathers her strength, resting just beyond physical reality, and prepares for her next move.

Fourteen

Rachel dialed Dalton's number as she stood outside the abandoned kickboxing studio. After several rings, his voicemail sounded.

"Dalton, Rachel. I've been trying to get a hold of you. We're about to start shooting again, and I want to hear those stories."

She sighed, hating herself for being so superstitious, but she couldn't help herself. In the days since Jay's death, she had let her imagination run wild. It seemed to her that too many unexplained events had happened for this to all be some sort of coincidence.

The door swung open, and Ward stuck his head out.

"We ready?"

She nodded and followed him inside. The cameras were set up. Nelson grinned as she entered. Either he was in better spirits or he planned on actually punching her to get his revenge on Ward for the other day. She reminded herself that he and Ward had made peace at Jay's funeral.

Everything will go smoothly, she thought.

● ● ●

She searches.

Moving through the set undetected, she scans her surroundings for something she can use to make a big spectacle.

She doesn't have to directly feed to be nourished.

Belief can do that.

Some working on the film have already begun to believe.

Even the one who woke her has started to doubt his firm belief in coincidence. And he gave her a name.

She feels all this, and it feeds her.

Along the wall, she sees several jugs of cleaners. She looks from the jugs to the wires attached to the lighting and camera equipment. She moves toward the jugs.

After today, there would be no doubt.

Only faith.

● ● ●

Ward called action, and again, Rachel led Nelson to the center of the room. He watched the scene through his camera with none of the anxiety of the previous shoot. The past few days had left him exhausted.

Funerals served as an unpleasant reminder of where Ward knew he would ultimately end up. In a box covered in dirt, forgotten. Burying someone several years younger than him heightened the difficulty.

While Rachel served as a source of stability, he had always counted on Jay to make him laugh and take his mind off shit. There had been times over the last few days where the urge to call Jay had sprung up. Then he would remember. He would never call Jay again. No more getting stoned and watching movies. No more sipping Rebel Reserve from a stainless flask. His friend was gone forever.

Now they were behind schedule. He had thought about pushing back production even further, but couldn't afford it. Time was money in any business, but even more so in the movies.

Rachel kissed Nelson, and the burly actor threw her to the ground. Thankfully, neither of them had missed a step over the last few days. He hoped they could do this in one take. He had a lot to shoot today to make up for lost time.

● ● ●

This time, Ward noted Nelson pulled his punch before connecting with Rachel's face. Still, when Nelson held her down and simulated thrusting into her, a knot tightened in Ward's stomach. At least he could hope to inspire the same reaction in his viewers.

Satisfied with the footage, he yelled, 'Cut.'

"Great job, you two." He turned to Devon. "How'd your footage look?"

"Looks good from here, boss."

He nodded. He almost called for Jay to bring him the script. That tightened the knot in his stomach. He called for the script without using anyone's name.

When he raised his head, he saw the fire.

●●●

It spread across the floor as if spilled. Cast and crew ran for the door, everything taught in school about remaining calm and evacuating in an orderly fashion forgotten at the sight of the blaze.

Ward grabbed his camera, scanned the room for Rachel. Something exploded, throwing more fire across the premises. Several people got caught in the burst. They screamed and tried to pat down the flames on their clothes.

Someone took Ward's hand. At its feminine touch, he thought it was Rachel. Marielle stood before him, the way he'd imagined her. Platinum blond hair. Skin as pale as bone. But the eyes were wrong. They shined like two silver coins.

He dropped his gaze to her other hand in time to watch her empty a jug of cleaner onto the floor. The liquid spilled toward the fire. Her face had changed. Her skin had gone the gray color of death. Dirt and blood clung to her hair. Pus leaked from split lips. One eye hung from its socket. The other still shined blinding silver.

No longer a dream image, she stood solid in front of him. Flesh and blood. Her touch as solid as his feet on the floor. He screamed and yanked his hand away.

"Bill." Rachel stood separated from him by a stream of fire. The specter of Marielle was gone. "Come on."

People struggled to get through the door. Screaming, trampling one another, pushing against the door frame. Ward bit his lip.

"We're not getting out that way," she said.

She held up one of the boom microphone stands and ran for the closest window. She smashed the stand against the glass, and Ward took one last look around the engulfed room. He wouldn't be able to save the lights, or the location, or the film. People would be hurt, probably even killed. An insurance nightmare loomed. He would be ruined.

Maybe it's better if I stay in here and burn.

The window shattered. "Come on, Bill, let's go."

She climbed onto the sill and checked over her shoulder. The sight of her eyes moved him. He ran, careful not to step in the fire, always watching for Marielle.

He spilled out the window, staggered across the parking lot, and collapsed.

Fifteen

Ward flipped through the pages of *Mania* in his lap. *Could these pages really be cursed? Did they kill Jay? Did they burn down our set?* He sat on his couch, unable to sit in his study without the weight of everything overwhelming him. Rachel sat beside him.

"You know, this isn't your fault," she said.

He flexed his fingers on the edges of the screenplay. Could he tell her what he had seen in the fire?

"What's to blame then? The curse?"

She stood up and crossed her arms, her expression difficult to read.

"What?" he said.

"Maybe that's not such a crazy idea."

He nodded. "I'm starting to think the same thing. When I was in the fire, I ..."

"You saw her?"

He bit his lip.

"I saw her too."

He set the script aside. "What? When?"

"The first day. When Alison was doing my makeup."

"Jesus. Why didn't you say something?"

She raised her eyebrows. "What could I say?"

"Yeah, I guess you have a point." He leaned back. "So, if this is a curse, what happens now?"

"Maybe it's over?"

"If the other people who tried to film this script died or went insane, I'd say you and I got off easy."

"Jay's dead. Julian quit. Some of our PAs and technicians are covered in burns. You don't think that's enough?"

"I don't know. We're done filming. We'll go bankrupt just trying to get it together again."

She crossed her arms. "We should find out what happened to the others."

"I still think this whole thing just sounds crazy."

"I know, Bill. Believe me. I'm not one to buy into this sort of thing, but with everything that's happened since you got your hands on *Mania*, I have a hard time believing this is all some kind of coincidence.

"You're not acting like you. We're seeing things that aren't there. And people are fucking dead. There has to be something else at work here."

"Well, the hallucinations and my mood could just be stress."

"But that doesn't explain Jay's death or the fire."

He thought about this. "Well, what do you think it is?"

"What if it's not a curse or a series of coincidences?"

"What does that leave?"

"What if someone is trying to sabotage us?"

"Who would want to do that?"

"I don't know, but we should try to find out."

Thinking of the series of events as coordinated by living, breathing people was a lot easier to swallow than curses and vengeful spirits. It didn't explain the hallucinations, or the vivid dreams, or his dark moods as of late, though.

And she touched you. Hallucinations can't touch you.

He shook the thought away. It had happened in the middle of a crisis. His stress had been so high during that fire, he would not have been shocked if he had seen Jesus Christ riding a pink tapir through the flames. Thinking of Jay, he swallowed a sob that wanted to burst free from his throat.

"All right," he said. "I can start with Mr. Whale. He sold me this damn script. I'm sure he knows something. How about you? Where are you going to start?"

"I'll do some reading, I guess. Dig up some old issues of the trades. See if there's anything weird in them."

He nodded, picked up the screenplay, and stood.

"What are you doing?"

"I'm going to light this fucking thing on fire."

"Lot of good that will do."

"What ... oh yeah. Copies."

Everyone on set had one.

Sixteen

Even in the daylight, Mr. Whale's home exuded an old world, haunted atmosphere. Ward drove up the cobblestone drive, through the yard of gargoyles, and parked in front of the arched doorway.

He had called Mr. Whale earlier in the day and insisted upon an appointment.

"All sales are final," the old man had said.

"I don't want a refund. I just need to ask you a few questions. Can I come by?"

"Of course, my boy. Any son of Stephen's is welcome in my abode."

Ward ignored the mention of his father and said he would be by in an hour.

Now, as he beat on the door, he half-expected the ghostly Marielle to answer, only not as a ghost. She and Mr. Whale would tell him it had all been an elaborate prank. His pride would suffer and so would his wallet, but at least Jay would still be alive and nobody would be hurt.

Mr. Whale opened the door. "Ah, William, how good it is to see you. May I offer you a drink?"

"I just want to talk. Can I come in?"

Mr. Whale pulled open the door and stood aside. "Of course."

"I need to know where you found *Mania*."

"I told you, I'd rather not—"

"Yeah, you'd rather not say. Well, I need to know." Ward injected a threatening tone to his words. He hated acting like a bully but needed answers. He expected his demeanor to upset Mr. Whale, but the old man's eyes softened.

"My dear boy, has something happened?"

"I'm sure it's in the trades today, but my production is fucking doomed. One of my PAs was murdered, and one of my locations burned down yesterday. I need to know what's going on and if someone is fucking with me."

"Come to my office. Standing too long can be quite taxing for me, I'm afraid."

Ward took a breath, not liking Whale's nonchalance but not wanting to say something that would ruin his chances of getting answers. "Sure."

They entered a room with a massive desk and walls lined with vintage movie posters. Whale sat in a leather chair, and Ward sat across from him.

"Has anything else happened?"

"You wouldn't believe me if I told you."

"Have you seen her? The actress from the script?"

Ward's stomach clenched.

"Marielle. I saw her as the location burned. Rachel, my lead, says she saw her too. First, she looked normal, then ..."

Mr. Whale nodded.

"Did you know about this?"

Mr. Whale shrugged. "I have heard the stories, but of course, I've never believed them. At their best, they're interesting coincidences. At their worst, they're nothing more than urban legends. I may be old, but I still have my wits about me."

"Then why don't you tell me how you got the script?"

He faced the wall, but Ward thought Mr. Whale was gazing somewhere even farther away.

"The second time it went into production, back in nineteen ninety-one, there was a detective who investigated the murders. Atkins, his name was. He was, is, a friend of mine. He knew about my interests in obscure cinematic artifacts, so he gave it to me as a gift."

"He gave you evidence?"

"It was hardly evidence, William. That would have required the Los Angeles Police Department to believe in the curse, which, of course, they don't."

"What else?"

"Productions were troubled. Both then and in eighty-seven. And now, apparently."

"What about details?"

"The main players either died or had nervous breakdowns." He shrugged. "Not much else to it."

"Can it be stopped?"

"You're serious? You believe the curse is real?"

"I don't know what I believe, but I definitely think there's more going on here than interesting coincidences."

"My God, boy."

Ward tried to think. If Mr. Whale knew as little as he claimed, then he wasn't such a useful source of information. "The detective, what did you say his name was?"

"Atkins. He's retired now."

"I need to get in contact with him."

"What will you say? I doubt you'll get far with him once you start telling him about ghosts and old curses."

"I have to try."

"Are you going to start filming again?"

"I doubt it. We lost a lot of money and a lot of time already."

"Then, if people were trying to sabotage your production, or even if this curse is real, what are you afraid of? Bad things only happened to people while the film was in production."

"Do you know that for sure? Because I don't. Please, I'll feel a lot better if I just knew more."

Mr. Whale's eyes glistened as he regarded Ward. "Okay, but only because of who you are. Your father—"

Ward slammed his hand on Mr. Whale's desk. "And you can stop telling me about my father. He may have meant a lot to you, but I hardly knew the guy. Making movies meant more to him than his family did. He wasn't around for my mom when she lost her shit and nearly killed herself, or for my brother when he got addicted, and he wasn't around for me when I needed someone to be. As far as I'm concerned, I hope he's rotting in hell as we speak."

Mr. Whale's soft expression remained unshaken by Ward's harsh words. He wrote a name and number on a notepad, tore off the sheet, and handed it to Ward.

"Thanks."

"Don't mention it. Just ... a word of advice?"

"All ears."

"Proceed with caution. You may think it's important to find answers, but when you've been around as long as I have, you learn that answers don't always grant you the relief you expect. Sometimes answers are worse than questions."

Seventeen

Rachel sat at a computer in the Frances Howard Goldwyn Regional Library. Though she hated to admit it to herself, she feared being home alone. She skimmed through old issues of the trades. From visiting the Hollywood Inferno forum, she found out which years to look through.

Back in 1987, *Mania* went into production under a first-time director named Ashton Smith. In interviews, he said he was given the script by someone special, someone whose work he admired, but didn't reveal that person's identity.

She saw Detrik cast as the male lead, a film director who takes the unnamed actress in and helps her find work, a collaboration that leads to an ill-fated romance. Detrik's work before the film had been roles usually designated for character actors. Random police officers. Tough guys in bars. Prisoners. *Mania* was set to be his first lead role.

Reading about Detrik made her think of Dalton. Talking directly to Detrik would reveal more information to her. The trades kept the details vague. Several cast and crew members died under mysterious circumstances. Ashton himself had a nervous breakdown and ended up in a catatonic state. She wondered if he was still alive. She wondered if she could get back issues of tabloids from the time. Those publications would be more shameless depicting the information.

Still, vague or not, reading about this scared her. It further convinced her that this couldn't be some coincidence. Other forces were at work, and she wasn't ready to rule out ghosts.

Rachel's mother had married an American businessman whose firm had dealings in Japan. Her father's influence had fostered in Rachel a material view of the world. Her maternal grandmother had a more mystical outlook. She told Rachel famous Japanese ghost stories like "The Spirit of the Willow Tree" and "Great Fire Caused by a Lady's Dress." Her grandmother never suggested these stories were fiction. They were important stories from her culture, and she believed them.

While Rachel had never bought their veracity, she now recalled those stories and her grandmother's unshakeable belief in them. In the face of the unexplained, she thought the idea of a larger world full of forces that influenced this one wasn't such a stretch.

Her phone vibrated in her purse. She got up and ducked into the hallway that led to the bathrooms. She saw answering her phone in the library as an unforgivable sin.

"Hello?"

"Rachel. Dalton."

"Dalton, can I see you?"

"Sure. I heard about what happened yesterday. How are you holding up?"

"I'm alive. There's that." She paused. "Can you bring Detrik with you?"

"I'll see what I can do."

"It's important."

A pause. "I'll make it happen."

"Good. Meet me at the Lexington Social House on Vine in an hour."

"I'll get recognized there."

"Like that ever bothers you."

She hung up and left the library.

Eighteen

Atkins lived in a studio apartment in a complex off of Fuller Avenue. Ward knocked on the door. A white-haired man with a healthy build and a thick mustache answered.

"You William?"

Ward stuck out his hand. "William Ward."

Atkins took Ward's hand into a meaty paw and shook. "Rory Atkins."

Once inside, Atkins motioned for Ward to have a seat at a small round table.

"I made some coffee," Atkins said. He went into the kitchen and emerged with two steaming mugs. He set one in front of Ward and sat down in the other chair. "Mr. Whale told me you'd be calling. You want to know about the *Mania* murders."

Ward nodded.

Atkins lit a cigarette. "Want one?"

Ward declined.

"We never did find out who was responsible for those killings. Never enough to go on."

"What actually happened?"

"First one to die was the art director. Found him in his house. No murder weapon."

"Suffocated?"

Atkins' face darkened. "Yes, but ..."

He took a pull from the cigarette and flicked ashes into an empty saucer.

"What?"

"Well, it was more than that. He was partially liquefied."

"Come on. Next you're gonna tell me there were two puncture wounds on his neck."

"No, nothing like that, but whatever stole his breath also made him bleed out."

What a strange way to put it: stole his breath. Ward thought about this. Had Jay and the girl, Tara, bled out like that too? There hadn't been anything written about that in the police reports or the newspapers.

"We made a conscious decision not to leak that bit of information to the press," Atkins said as if reading Ward's mind.

"Why?"

Atkins coughed and took a swig of coffee to lubricate his throat. "Are you kidding? They would've had a field day with that. Probably would've started talking about stakes and garlic. That kinda shit. You know how they are."

Ward nodded. Even though his films had never reached a wide audience, he had sure felt famous seven years ago when his steady relationship with actress Charlotte Bright fell apart. She had left him for A-list director Brad Winn, and the press had been diligent invading his privacy.

"So, we kept it out of the papers," Atkins said, "even when it happened again and again. Two cast members, Holly Sposato and Carl Boyd, were killed in the same way. The producer Jared Warner. Last to go was the director, Jean-Paul Ross.

"We did look back at the first time *Mania* went into production, but other than the murders and the screenplay, we didn't see a connection."

"You didn't think that was weird?"

"Weird how? You don't think it had to do with the script, do you?"

Ward kept a poker face.

"I hope not. I dealt with enough of you kooks back then. People need to see connections between everything. They need to know someone's in charge, even if that someone is a murdering psychopath."

"I don't know about a connection. I'm merely curious. The screenplay's being shot again. I'm shooting it. I kind of ..."

"Want to exploit the murders for publicity? Shit, man, you people will do anything to get your movie seen."

"It's nothing like that."

"Yeah, sure." Disgust dripped off of Atkins's every word.

"Anyway, did you have any suspects?"

"Nope." Atkins sniffed and leaned back in his chair.

"I just have one more question."

Atkins lit another smoke with the remains of the first, took a deep drag, and exhaled in Ward's face. "Go ahead."

"Did the killings stop when production stopped?"

"Well, no. Production stopped once Holly died. She was the lead, and they had to recast her. The killings didn't stop until the director died. Whoever did it ..."

Atkins sighed. Ward waited for him to complete the thought.

"Whoever did it wanted to make a point."

Nineteen

Rachel entered the Lexington and scoped the place for Dalton. He sat in a booth against the wall, facing the floor of the establishment. A bulky, dark-haired male sat across the table clutching a mug of beer in his hands. She did not relish the idea of sitting next to Dalton, but the man she assumed was Detrik made her even more uncomfortable. She slid in beside her former costar.

"Rachel, meet Mark Detrik. Mark, this is Rachel Katayama."

Detrik regarded her with hooded eyes. He spoke in a soft, low voice. "I've seen your short films. You've got a lot of talent."

"Thanks."

As she examined the aged actor up and down, she only vaguely recognized him. She found it hard to believe that he had been slated to play the lead in the first incarnation of Mania, but guessed the last twenty-seven years had simply not been kind to him.

"So, you're supposed to be in *Mania*?"

"I was. We had to shut things down for the time being. It's all up in the air." She paused, then added. "I was slated to play the female lead."

His shadowed eyes widened. "Marielle."

"You know her name?"

He stared into the fizzing glass of beer. "We lost our leading lady. It wasn't pretty."

"What happened?"

"Same shit that will happen to you if you're not careful."

Rachel's jaw dropped. Dalton burst into laughter.

"See, Rachel, I told you this guy was great."

Detrik glared at Dalton. "I'm serious. Every few years, someone gets it in their head to shoot that damn script, and it's always a bad fucking idea."

"Then why are you still alive?"

He dwelt on this for a minute, stared off into space. "I'm important, I guess."

"What does that mean?"

"I'm only guessing."

Dalton giggled behind his hand, and Rachel wanted to slap him.

"Important for what?"

"I think whatever this force is thrives on people believing in it. Someone like me who spreads the gospel, so to speak, is important."

"So you believe in the curse?"

"Sure as hell do."

"Wait," Dalton said. "Rachel, are you telling me you believe this?"

She stared hard at him. "I don't know. I'm running out of options, Dalton. If you would've seen what I've seen ..."

"Barked up the wrong tree with you."

She stayed focused on Detrik. "Does this mean you're giving it power now? By telling me these stories?"

Detrik shrugged.

"Tell me."

"We lost a few cast members. The last to die was our female lead, Claudia Rossetti. The director, Ashton Smith, didn't die, but we definitely lost him."

"What happened to him?"

"After Claudia died, suffocated like everyone else, we had to shut down production. We had money behind us though, so the producer wanted to recast Marielle and get the ball rolling again soon. Only no one could get a hold of Ashton. He wouldn't answer his phone. The producer finally went to Ashton's house and kicked in the door.

"He noticed a foul smell as soon as he reached the house. The upholstered chairs in the living room were slashed open, garbage was strewn about the floor, and every mirror in the house had been smashed."

Dalton had stopped laughing. Rachel guessed he hadn't heard this part of the story before.

"Strange shit was written on the walls, a bunch of cryptic messages, Marielle's name over and over.

"They found Ashton stripped naked in the bathroom, kneeling in his own filth. More of that strange writing was painted on his torso with blood and shit. He was emaciated, but alive. Found his eyes in the sink."

"Oh my God," she said.

"Yum," Dalton said without humor.

"Where is he now?"

"He's up at Hillview in Pacoima. He's been catatonic since they found him."

"That was almost thirty years ago," Dalton said.

Detrik nodded.

Dalton leaned back. "Shit."

"How do I stop this?" Rachel asked.

Detrik's eyes softened. She looked from him to Dalton. Detrik said nothing more.

"I need to go," she said. "Thanks for meeting me, Dalton."

"That's it?" He looked at Detrik. "Should she be worried?"

Detrik put his head down.

Rachel nodded. "I'll handle it, Dalton."

Dalton stood up. "The fuck you will. I'm gonna help you. It might not be a curse, but something fucked up is definitely going on."

"I said I'll handle it. No sense in dragging you into this."

"But, Rachel ..."

She turned to Detrik. "One more thing: where did Ashton get that screenplay?"

Detrik met her gaze. "It was given to him by Stephen Ward."

Twenty

Ward's skin had gone pale, and bloodshot cracks split his eyes. Rachel embraced him, enjoying the feel of his arms, regardless of what the future might hold. They broke apart and sat down in their respective chairs.

Ward told her that Mr. Whale had not been particularly helpful and while the detective had given him plenty of history, he didn't give a whole lot of information that helped them. He mentioned the loss of fluids as well as the suffocation.

"Gross."

"How did your reading go?"

"I was able to find out a little, but then I got a call from Dalton."

"Dalton?"

"Well, he said he could introduce me to Mark Detrik who worked on the first production of *Mania*."

"So you went to see him?"

"Bill, I'm trying to help us. I had to use whatever resources I had."

Ward bit his lip. "Did anything happen between you two when you worked on that film together?"

"Seriously? Is that what's on your mind right now?"

"I'd like to know."

"Nothing happened. I told you. Whatever relationship I have with him is harmless. Do you believe me?"

He gazed at his shoes.

"You don't believe me."

"Just tell me what you found out."

She wanted to press the issue further, but decided against it. They had more important things to worry about.

"Detrik said the death of the lead actress caused them to shut down production. Before they could recast her, the director ... well, he's in a mental hospital now. Catatonia."

"At least he lived, I guess. The second director wasn't so lucky. What else did you find out?"

"I found out how Ashton Smith got his hands on the script for *Mania*."

"Someone gave it to him, right? Someone Ashton Smith admired. Do you know who it was?"

"You're not gonna like it."

Ward bit his lip. He searched his thoughts, explored the darkest places within him. "It was my father, wasn't it?"

She nodded. "Yeah."

"It makes sense it would be him."

"How so?"

"I remember him talking about a secret project he had in the works when I was a kid. Said it was going to change everything. And the old guy who gave us the screenplay admires the hell out of him too. Dad's been this constant shadow over my life. Of course he'd be connected to my undoing."

She put a firm hand on Ward's knee. "Hey, this isn't going to be your undoing. We're gonna figure this out."

He took in her words and peered into her dark eyes. He thought he never loved her more than he did now. Thoughts of his father turned the moment sour.

"All right, so what do we do now?" he asked, more than happy to hand control over to her. His skin had grown hot, and a sensation like he was being choked tightened around his throat while he waited for her answer.

"We'll go to your grandmother's. She's bound to have some of your father's things. Maybe she has something that can give us a clue as to what we're up against."

Something like hairy spider legs crawled up Ward's arms. He didn't want to go forward. He wanted to get in his car and drive aimlessly, away from home, away from everything. But Rachel was right. They couldn't give up. When he thought about how hard he had fought to stay alive during the darker periods of his life—the aftermath of his mother's attempted suicide, her eventual death from lung cancer, and the black hole of depression that swallowed him following the production on *The Mouth of Hell*—he had to keep moving.

Twenty-One

Dalton Carver sat in a private room at a dive karaoke bar in West Hollywood. He had given the waiter a generous tip to keep the drinks coming and to have the room to himself. He shut off the karaoke machine and sat in the dark, drinking an extra dirty martini.

Fucking Rachel. Not only does she give me the cold shoulder, she turns out to be batshit crazy.

He was not used to rejection. Women—and sometimes men—threw themselves at his feet. Rachel had been so wrapped up in what Detrik had to say. Of course, Detrik had told a compelling story. For a moment there, even Dalton had bought it. Once he had done some thinking, he realized how crazy the whole thing sounded.

Rachel and her no-talent boyfriend had just run into a string of bad luck. Nothing more.

Still, he couldn't help feeling bummed about not getting a chance to ask Rachel out again.

He would have started as before, asking her for an innocent drink. This time, he wouldn't have taken 'no' for an answer. They would have gone out as friends, but he would have charmed her. Worn her down. She would have forgotten about her two-bit indie filmmaker boyfriend in no time.

A lost cause now. He didn't usually mind crazy. Lord knew he had dated his share of crazy. Rachel, though, was something special. Dalton could handle bipolar broads or sexual deviants, but someone who believed in ghosts and curses? Too much for Dalton Carver. She had not outright stated she believed in that shit, but she didn't deny it either. Probably some weird Asian thing. Either way, no thanks.

Now he needed to collect himself. Drinking helped. Being alone did too, if only for a little while. What he really needed was a good piece of ass. Not just any piece of ass. He had numerous phone numbers of women he could turn to for that. No, Dalton needed a new piece of ass, the piece of ass equivalent to a new car smell.

He peeked out behind the curtains of his private room to scope out the bar scene. Lot of pretty faces, but nothing special. He took a gulp of his drink and grimaced.

He took one more look around the bar, not hoping for much, but stopped.

A blond sat alone at a high table near the window. She stared out into the dark street. Even with her face half-hidden, she drew his attention. How had he missed her before? Her pale flesh glowed in the dimly lit bar. She wore a black dress that clung to her in a way that showed every curve and angle. She sat straight, with confidence, but also carried a mystique that Dalton could not quite explain.

The biggest mystery: why had no guy approached her yet? Dalton fancied that only he saw her. That she was there just for him, on a night he was feeling down in the dumps.

When his next martini arrived, he slipped the waiter a twenty dollar bill and asked him to get the blond a drink. The waiter checked across the bar. He turned back to Dalton. Confusion creased his face.

"Where did you say she was sitting?"

Dalton walked up to the curtain and parted it. He pointed, but no one sat in the high table by the window.

"She was just there. Goddamn it."

"I'm sorry, Mr. Carver."

He groaned and waved him out of the room. He slammed his martini in two gulps and gnashed the olives between his teeth. He swallowed and headed for the exit.

Outside, he saw no trace of the blond.

Guess it's not my night.

He called for a ride.

● ● ●

When his car pulled up in front of his house, the blond was sitting on his front steps, hands folded between her knees and gazing off to the side as if posing for a photograph.

"Boss, did you call for her?" the driver asked.

"No."

"Want me to call the police?"

Dalton smirked at the driver. "I think I can handle one little lady, don't you?"

"Sure, boss."

She sat still and silent, smiled when Dalton approached.

"Hey," she said.

"Hey, yourself, how did you find me?"

"I was looking for you."

A notion that the woman could be crazy entered his mind, but the night was coming to an end, and he needed to get laid.

"Well, here I am, beautiful." He took a bow. "I tried to buy you a drink, but you already left. How about we rectify that? I've got a sweet bar inside."

"I'm sure it's very impressive."

"Well, what do you say?"

"I'm here, aren't I? Now you just have to let me in."

He winked at her, walked up the steps, and she followed.

Twenty-Two

Solomon Grant hung up his phone and looked at the sprawling, heavily windowed mansion beside him. Dalton must've been on quite the bender last night for him to sleep through four phone calls. Solomon should've known better than to leave him with that girl. Dalton had to be on the set of a cologne commercial in half an hour, and Solomon couldn't get in touch with him.

Fucking beautiful. He thought back to fifteen years ago when he had first come to Hollywood with a script to sell. After finding work as a chauffeur, he had put the project on hold and never gone back. On days like today, he regretted that decision. No, he thought. Regret isn't strong enough. Grief. He grieved the decision to put his artistic endeavor on the backburner to pursue his driving career. Now he was stuck carting around celebrities with gargantuan egos and sleeping schedules as erratic as a meth-addicted cat's. Most of his clients sucked, but Dalton was by far the worst. If he wasn't such a generous tipper, there had been numerous occasions where Solomon would have hauled off and punched the asshole in the mouth.

Once, Dalton had not been able to get a hold of his regular drug dealer but had wanted to score some cocaine in order to impress his date for the night. He made Solomon drive way the fuck out to East Sunset Boulevard to buy blow from some scumbag off the streets. The worst part: Solomon had to do the actual transaction because Dalton was afraid of getting recognized.

That night, Solomon had almost forgotten about how well Dalton paid him. This morning presented the same level of annoyance, because it would not be Dalton who got chewed out if he missed the shoot. No, it would be Solomon. Somehow it would be Solomon's fault that Dalton was too wasted to answer his phone and get driven around.

Solomon got out of the car. Not today. Dalton was gonna have to man up and get his ass in the car. Solomon didn't care how hungover Dalton was. He banged his fist on the front door and jabbed the doorbell.

"Dalton. You in there? Check out time, man."

He pounded on the door again, listened. Nothing. Was Dalton even home? That would be just peachy-tangerine-y if he and that girl had taken off somewhere without telling anyone. Solomon looked around at his feet. He stuck his key in the door lock and turned. No alarm sounded when he opened the door. Dalton must have been too sloshed to even remember that last night.

For having such a large house, Dalton didn't have a lot of things. Expensive furniture, sure, but not a whole lot else. Solomon checked around for anything out of the ordinary.

"Dalton?"

He did a quick search of the living room and kitchen before heading upstairs. Solomon didn't relish the idea of having to see Dalton and that girl in bed naked together, but it was either that or he would get chewed out by some hack TV commercial director.

Solomon noticed the stink as soon as he started down the hallway. Like shit buried in sugar. He pressed his hand against his nose and mouth, trying to breathe as little as possible. He increased his pace.

He opened the door to Dalton's master bedroom, and the smell overpowered him. He gagged, and in mid-dry-heave, something grabbed hold of him.

His attacker was an emaciated form, its eyes so far back in their sockets Solomon could hardly see them. Brittle, skeletal hands held him. The fingers that didn't snap off dug grooves into his shoulders. The form opened its mouth and expelled a belch of rancid air. It spoke, its voice a choked rasp.

"Solomon, help ... it's me, Dalton."

Solomon screamed and backed away from the malformed remains that claimed to be the once vibrant Dalton Carver. The withered body advanced on him.

"Please ... Solomon ..." Maggots poured from between his lips.

Solomon continued to back down the hallway. "Get the hell away from me, man. Just stay back. I'll call for help."

"Help me." Gray flaps of skin fell from his bottom jaw. One eye popped, spewing something like egg yolk flecked with blood. He opened his mouth again, and black drool leaked from his purple, withered lips. "Please."

The thing that used to be Dalton lunged forward, and Solomon stepped to the side. The wasted body tumbled headlong down the stairs. Bones snapped with every impact as the body rolled and flipped, coming to rest at the foot of the staircase. A puddle of yellow and black fluid oozed across the surrounding floorboards.

Solomon stared down at the wet pile of bones and ashen flesh.

"Fuck," he said. The day's shit quotient had just taken a dramatic leap.

Twenty-Three

Rachel slurped the last of her tea. She didn't feel cold, but the heat offered comfort. Her hands on the heated mug connected her to something solid and tangible. Something warm. It helped her think.

Ward's grandmother, Lucille, stood at the edge of the kitchen, a small-framed woman with a head full of white curls. She couldn't see or hear too well, but those impediments didn't stop the woman from making a fantastic cup of tea. Rachel liked the quietude of the house. The trees and wildlife outside made the light and sound pollution of Los Angeles seem like a bad dream.

"Is William okay?" Lucille asked. He was sleeping upstairs.

Rachel considered Lucille's question. "He's shaken up from the last few days, but yeah, I think he's okay."

"I mean, really okay."

Rachel blinked. "I don't know what you mean."

The older woman's cloudy gray eyes stared down Rachel. "I think you do."

Rachel didn't answer.

"Stephen did a lot of damage to him," Lucille said. "William ... well, you were with him when he got sick a few years ago."

Rachel didn't want to think about this now. They had enough on their plates. But what if it was connected somehow? What if Marielle preyed on him because of his weaknesses? That didn't explain why others were killed, though.

"He's holding together, all things considered," Rachel said.

"What sort of trouble are you two in?"

"The truth?"

Lucille raised an eyebrow.

"The truth is we don't really know. We were hoping ... do you have anything of Stephen's?"

"I have a lot of his things. My husband couldn't bring himself to get rid of them after Stephen died, and after my husband died, I couldn't bring myself to throw them out either."

"What all do you have?"

"I've never really looked through it. You and William are more than welcome to do so. Does what's happening involve Stephen somehow?"

"That's what we hope to find out."

●●●

Ward rolled onto his side. Being home offered none of the comfort it once had. His grandmother's house used to be somewhere he would go to clear his head. He had spent a great deal of time here during the dark months that followed *The Mouth of Hell*. Now his mind refused to clear. His thoughts and fears ran rampant.

He thought back to the fire. She had the opportunity to kill him then. They had stood so close to each other, flames engulfing their surroundings. Yet she hadn't, and he couldn't figure out why.

He opened his Flipboard app to browse the news stories, thinking that would help him relax. The headline on the front page made him gasp.

ACTOR DALTON CARVER FOUND DEAD IN HOME

He skimmed the article for details. Apparently, Dalton had fallen down the stairs, but according to his chauffeur, he had been sick. Authorities suspected some kind of drug. Other than that, details were scant. The restrained reporting reminded him of the reports surrounding the *Mania* murders, and he wondered if there was some kind of connection.

He shuddered at the thought. Ward didn't like the actor's fixation on Rachel. In fact, he didn't like the actor at all, but he didn't want him dead. Even if he was more on edge than usual over the last few weeks, wishing someone dead in a jealous rage was out of character for him. When he looked inward, though, something ugly stared back. Had he orchestrated this somehow?

Why didn't she kill me in the fire? She could have killed me in the fire.

Footsteps padded up the stairs. "Bill?"

He closed the article and sat up as Rachel entered.

"Did you sleep?"

"I couldn't."

"I don't blame you."

"So what's up?" he asked, pushing Dalton out of his mind.

"Your grandmother says a bunch of your father's things are up in the attic. Did you want to come take a look with me?"

"Yeah, sure." He got out of bed and put on his shoes. He would tell her about Dalton later.

• • •

They started with the biggest box, unpacking things like childhood photographs and paintings done in elementary school. Ward found it hard to imagine his father as a little boy. The man had been born old. All of Ward's life, his father had been a successful blockbuster filmmaker. Like the rest of the world, Ward knew him from his movies alone.

After rooting through seven boxes, Ward and Rachel sat in the stuffy attic, sweaty and not any closer to figuring out what they were dealing with and how his father was connected.

"I can't believe it," she said. "Not a fucking thing in these boxes about Marielle or *Mania* or anything."

"So what now?"

She threw up her hands and stomped on the ground. A board popped up and hit Ward in the nuts.

He clutched his genitals and bowed. "Oh, fuck."

Rachel put her hand on his shoulder. "Oh my God, I'm so sorry."

Ward stared at the loose board, his eyes blurry. When the pain subsided, he crawled toward the opening. He dug his fingers into the seam and pulled the board all the way up.

"Is anything down there?"

"Hand me your lighter."

She passed it to him. He held it down between the boards and flicked it. The fire illuminated a fifteen-by-twelve-inch wooden box.

"Something's down there. Another box." He released the lighter and brought his hand back up. "See if Grandma's got a toolbox somewhere. We have to get some of these boards up."

Rachel nodded and went downstairs. Ward checked the dark gap where the loose board had been. Why hadn't it also been nailed down? Did someone intend for this box to be eventually found?

Rachel returned with a small plastic kit and placed it on the floor beside Ward. He took out a hammer and began pulling up the nails. A few moments later, he held the wooden box in his hands. A bright crimson carving of a serpent curled around a hammer decorated the box's lid. Two hinges and a latch kept the lid attached to the base.

He tried to pry the lid open with his hands, but the latch resisted. Using a flathead screwdriver proved more effective. Inside the box, several papers and photographs sat below a small black book.

A stone with an eye painted on it rested in the corner of the box. He and Rachel exchanged glances.

Rachel lifted the book out of the box and revealed the top photograph. Ward gasped at the instant recognition. The woman in the photo had blond hair that fell across her shoulders in layers. Dark makeup bordered her soft blue eyes. Her lips were slightly parted as if preparing to speak or plea.

Rachel examined the photo. "Oh my God, it's her."

Ward's eyes drifted to the right-hand corner of the photograph. Red lipstick marks and the words, "For you," written below indicated that this had been some kind of gift.

Rachel opened the book.

"It's a journal," she said.

"What's it say?"

Rachel began to read.

●●●

I see her, and I know she's perfect.

So tragic: a beautiful thing like her walking in the rain. She's lost and downtrodden, but she has purpose. Or at least wants purpose. Why else would she be in this town?

I take her in and ask her to stay. Though I'm confident she's right, I have to be absolutely sure. She doesn't know it, but it's an interview. An audition.

Does she deserve to be worshipped?

She tells me about her family. She has no contact with them, and neither party has attempted to reach out. Both parents have a history of heavy methamphetamine use. Both parents were physically and verbally abusive. She ran away from their home in Hot Springs, Arkansas to escape. She came to Hollywood because movies were the only thing to which she connected while growing up. She has a strong affinity for films featuring strong, yet tragic, females: *Sugarland Express*, *All About Eve*, and *The Uninvited*. She worked the streets to keep herself fed and auditioned whenever she could.

As she sits with me in the bed we've just shared, she believes that I can save her. She won't be saved in the way she expects.

I tell my brothers about her as soon as I'm sure she's fallen asleep. I tell them everything she's told me, and they agree that she may be a good candidate.

●●●

"Candidate for what?" Ward asked.

Rachel shrugged.

"Read more."

She skimmed over the next few entries. "It looks like they became close. Intimate. He promised her a role in his next big film, gave her a place to stay, and listened to her. Just like in the screenplay. He bought her jewelry. Your dad sounds like a real charmer."

Ward grunted.

Rachel skimmed over more pages of Stephen courting Marielle, making her feel comfortable and loved. She stopped on the last sentence of one entry and read it aloud: "I can tell she trusts me. This makes what I'll do to her all the more difficult, but I have to remember I'm doing something wonderful for her. I must keep my resolve, my faith. I'm giving her what she's always wanted."

Ward balled his hands into fists. "I thought nothing else about my father could surprise me, but I have a feeling he's the one that kills her and that ..." He shook his head. "Fuck."

She tried to offer a sympathetic smile, but it felt like a grimace. Stephen Ward had done a number on his lover's psyche, and reading the man's journal just showed how little he had cared about other people. Here he had manipulated this poor, broken woman into thinking he loved her, plotted to kill her, and acted like he was doing her some kind of favor. The man was a sociopath. Despite the damage he'd done to Bill by not being around, it was a blessing Bill hadn't been raised by him.

"Keep reading," he said.

"Are you sure?"

He nodded. "We have to know what this is all about."

● ● ●

My brothers tell me that it's time. Break her heart, drive her to the brink of despair. Then, when she's almost given up hope, call her back with the promise of reconciliation, and kill her. It must happen this way. It's all necessary for the resurrection to work.

If you're reading this, you must think I'm a monster, but consider this: I've seen people die and rise again as gods.

It shall be the same for her. You'll know her when she's gone. You'll love her when she's gone. Her name will be whispered in this town's dark alleys. People will die for her.

● ● ●

It's done. I'm not supposed to give any details, even in my own journal, but I will say she's dead now. Her story has been written in the form of a screenplay and will be passed along to someone to film it.

Ashton Smith is perfect. A young up-and-comer, he has something to say. He still believes he can make something to shift the cosmos. That conviction is necessary to bring her story to life, but it won't be filmed. It will occur behind the scenes, as it has since the beginning.

Marielle isn't the first, and she won't be the last.

● ● ●

Rachel closed the book. "It links him to the first production, and he confesses to Marielle's murder. Maybe we can go to the police."

"They're not going to want to hear any ghost stories."

"True, but maybe it will link up with other pieces of evidence they have. Maybe they can expose these brothers or whoever your father was involved with."

Ward shook his head. "Even so, that's not going to stop Marielle from wanting us dead. All the police in the world can't help us there."

"What if breaking up the cult takes away her power?"

"Sounds too easy. Just because they'd be behind bars doesn't mean they'll stop believing. Also, these people might be untouchable. If they've been operating behind the scenes for long enough, there's no telling how wide their influence is. They might be above the law."

"What if there's a reason she wants us alive." Rachel asked.

"Like what?"

"I don't know, but why hasn't she come for us yet?

"Given she had a relationship with your father, it makes a strange sort of sense. Beyond that, I'm out of ideas. What about you?"

"I'm not sure going to the police is such a good idea yet. Maybe we should go see Atkins. See what he thinks. If he still has friends on the force, he may be able to use the journal to reopen the old cases and connect it to the current one."

"All right," she said. "I'm in."

Twenty-Four

They showed up without calling. Atkins opened the door for them, eyes narrowed.

"Sorry to intrude, but we found something you may want to take a look at."

"Take it to the police. I don't have time for more superstitious talk."

"No superstitions, no ghosts. Just facts." Ward held out the box.

At the sight of the symbol on the box's lid, Atkins's eyes widened. "Where did you find that?"

"It belonged to my father, Stephen Ward."

"Do you know what that symbol is?" Rachel asked.

Atkins frowned and shook his head. "No, I thought it looked familiar for a second, but I was wrong. Come on in. I'll take a look at whatever's inside, but this better not be a waste of my time."

"It won't be."

Atkins let them in. "I was about to make some tea. Would either of you like some?"

"I'm good," Ward said.

"Sure, I'll have a cup," Rachel said.

"Great. Have a seat in the living room. I'll be out shortly."

● ● ●

As Atkins filled the teapot, he picked up his phone and dialed a number he knew from memory. Someone picked up, but said nothing.

"It's Atkins. You'll never believe who just showed up in my apartment."

"I'll send someone over. You just keep them talking."

Atkins hung up, shut off the water, and put the pot on the stove. He cast a glance into the living room at Ward and Rachel. He thought for a moment that fate had been kind to him.

No, not fate. We did this. This is our design. Our grand production.

He opened a drawer and pulled out his revolver.

●●●

Atkins returned carrying two cups of tea. He handed one to Rachel and sat down.

"So, tell me what you've found."

Ward handed him the box. Atkins opened it and lifted out the journal. He set it aside and flipped through the photographs. He took the rock with the eye painted on it, held it up. "Cute."

"Most of what you'll want is in the journal."

Atkins picked it up. "What's actually in here?"

They told him what they knew. Atkins skimmed the first few pages.

"Do you have any friends left on the force who you can give this to?" Ward asked. "Maybe there's some way to tie it to what's happened every time *Mania* went into production."

"If the evidence proves compelling enough, I'm sure there's someone who would be interested in seeing it. I can understand why you came to me first, though."

"What makes you say that?" Ward asked.

"Well, first you come to me asking about the curse of your little film. Now, you come to me with this business about your father and some kind of cult." He held the book up and tossed it aside. "You've got quite an imagination, the both of you, but I think vengeful ghosts and shadowy groups operating behind the scenes in Hollywood are more like something you'd find in a film. We're in reality, my friends. While there may be a connection between the sets of murders, I'm sure there is a logical explanation."

"I don't buy it," Rachel said.

"Buy what?"

She rose to her feet.

"You know more than you're letting on. What aren't you telling us?"

"Sweetie, I haven't the foggiest idea what you mean."

"How about we make that the last time you call me 'sweetie,' and you can tell us what you're hiding?"

He laughed at her and turned to Ward. "You probably should have left this one tied up in the yard."

"What the hell?" Ward said. "You can't just say shit like that."

"That's it. Bill, we're getting out of here. Atkins, you just give us the box and the journal, and we'll take it to the police on our own. They'll have to believe us. We'll make them, somehow."

"How about the two of you stay put?"

"Um, how about we don't?" Rachel reached for the journal.

Atkins dug into his pants and pulled out a silver revolver.

"Shit." Ward took Rachel's hand and eased her back into her seat. He tried to think of something to say to convince Atkins not to shoot them, but facing down the barrel of a gun has a way of making you shut up.

Rachel squeezed his hand.

Someone knocked at the door.

Atkins smiled. "Looks like my other guests are here."

Atkins backed toward the door, never taking his eyes or the gun off of Ward and Rachel. Ward's body tensed as the door unlocked and swung open. Three men entered. One wore a dark business suit on a wiry frame. He resembled a corporate banker more than anything. The other two men could have been bouncers from any bar on Sunset Boulevard. All meat and bulk, with intense stares that could wither even the most fearless people Ward knew. They stood on either side of the businessman wearing smug grins. Ward could read their minds. They were about to do the kind of work they did best, and for these guys, there was no greater feeling than that of a job well done.

"Who are you? What the hell do you want?" Rachel said, showing none of the fear Ward felt.

The businessman turned toward the beast on his right and nodded. The hulk of a man crossed the room to Rachel and backhanded her across the face. She fell to the floor, conscious but visibly dazed.

"What the fuck?" Ward started to rise.

The man turned to Ward, the intense stare still burning in his eyes. Ward sat back down. The hulk held his position over Ward. The close-up sight of the man's muscles and the knowledge of just how badly he could damage Ward with them brought a wave of nausea.

"Atkins, my friend," the well-dressed man said, "you've done well. William, you haven't done so badly yourself. You woke Marielle and set this whole thing in motion."

The other brute left the businessman's side and began to pack up the contents of the box.

"Every generation needs its monster, and Marielle's time is just about finished. It's time for a new one to come forth."

"What are you going to do?"

"Well, since death and resurrection are how all gods are made, we're here to help you along."

"Me?" Ward asked.

"Why not? You're estranged from your family. You feel unful-filled, unloved. If you died now, it'd be in a fit of rage. You'd have to rise, like Marielle and others before her, to carve out your own bloody legacy."

Ward tried to wrap his mind around the businessman's words. He wanted to run, but he couldn't leave Rachel, and the beast of a man standing over him offered little room to maneuver.

"Or, maybe you're not the right one. Maybe Rachel would serve us better. She's certainly more interesting than you. She's got experience from both sides of the Pacific. And, of course, she's a lot prettier. We've been doing this for a long time, and women always make better sacrifices, more interesting stories. There's something more tragic about them when they die, isn't there? It seems wrong on a different level than if you kill a man."

The businessman signaled to the brute standing over Ward. Two monstrous hands clamped onto the sides of Ward's head. The man's knee struck Ward in the face. He fell back against the sofa, blinding white lights flashing in front of his eyes, blood filling his mouth. The brute took hold of him again and threw him to the floor.

What happened next only came to Ward in pieces. Rachel protested as one of the brutes lifted her off the ground and dragged her out of the room. A few more kicks struck Ward's ribs, but he hardly felt them. He distanced himself from his body as it was pummeled, the only thing he could be thankful for at the moment.

"Leave him," the businessman said. "Let Marielle finish him."

"And what am I supposed to do?" Atkins said.

"Leave for a while and come back. I'm sure she won't take long."

"How do you know she'll come at all?"

"She'll come. She's been looking for him."

He clapped Atkins on the shoulder and walked to the door. Atkins followed, leaving Ward behind in the dark.

Twenty-Five

Ward woke coughing blood. He spat out a wad of congealed crimson. His ribs and face throbbed in all the places he'd been hit. At least he knew he was still alive. Marielle had never shown.

His first attempt at getting to his feet ended with him collapsing back to the floor. He wondered just how badly he was hurt. Could these injuries kill him? He tried again, using the couch for support. He groaned as the pain spread across his body.

He wondered as he sat in the dark if now, in this moment, that businessman and the others were killing Rachel. How badly would she break down? Would she cry out to him? Or God?

He didn't want her to suffer, but knew she would.

The futility of any action he could take pressed down upon him, made him cry in the dark. It crushed his will to live.

He cursed and pounded the ground of the apartment. Fresh pain bloomed in his hand, and warm blood drizzled from his knuckles. He examined his wounds with morbid fascination. Poked at the scrapes on his hand, flexed his fingers, and caused more blood to pour. The outward pain dulled the inward despair.

He slammed his fist into the ground again. This time he grunted against it. He thought he broke a finger. He thought about pain as a doorway, about weakness leaving the body.

Back when he suffered from depression, he had once cut himself too deep and had to go to the hospital. Rachel had gone with him and taken him home after he had been cleared by the doctors. She had held him, made him promise that he wouldn't give up, told him she loved him and didn't want to lose him. Remembering this now brought a rush of tears. She hadn't given up on him, so how could he give up on her now?

He thought of Marielle sparing him in the fire. He shook his head. If she cared about him, why had she killed Jay? He remembered the screenplay and who she had been before she became a monster. She had been alone, desperate, and afraid, like he was now. She had been turned into a monster, but maybe pieces of her old self still remained.

He had never been a praying man. Religion had no place in his family. Even his grandparents had a greater interest in the arts than in religion. Now, he imagined himself as a devout man who still cried out to God, even after God had killed his loved ones or given him a crippling disease. Marielle had killed his friends and set these dark events in motion. But maybe she could help. He had called her before by working on the film. Perhaps she'd hear his call again.

"Marielle." He kept his voice at a whisper as he repeated her name.

Ward pressed his fists into his forehead. He shut his eyes. He called to her again and again, tried to picture her.

Panic rose within him as time passed. He thought of Ashton Smith, the doomed director who had previously tried to bring *Mania* to the screen. Ashton had gone crazy calling for her. Ward wondered if the circumstances were the same.

"Marielle, please, I need your help, Goddamn it."

He rose to his feet, dull aches pounding his ribs. "Please, don't let them hurt Rachel."

Ward turned to find her with him. He opened his mouth to scream, but her kiss swallowed it whole.

● ● ●

Instead of the life draining from him, energy poured into him. The pain from his wounds became sources of strength. Redness filled his vision, as if blood poured down the lenses of his eyes. The throb of his heart grew stronger with every beat, pumped fire through his veins.

Marielle pulled her lips from his, pulling him from one dream to another. The first had been raw sensation, elevated to its absolute peak. In this new dream, his perceptions changed yet again. His flesh tingled. His pain had dulled. An iron gate rippled like a reflection in water.

They were in front of Mr. Whale's mansion. Ward had a gun in his hand.

"How did we ...?"

"Just follow me," she said.

Her body oozed through the bars and reformed as flesh on the other side. He stared.

"Come on," she said.

"You killed all of my friends. You tried to kill me."

"It was the curse. I couldn't stop it."

"Why help me now?"

"They want to replace me. I won't allow them."

"And after we've stopped them, what then? You go back to trying to kill me? Trying to kill Rachel?"

Her eyes darkened. "I don't know the future. But right now, you need my help."

He nodded and stepped forward, through the iron. It felt like something reached inside him and massaged his organs. No pain in it.

Ward followed Marielle up the cobblestone path. The gargoyles turned their heads to watch the intruders, eyes glowing red, mouths twisted into jagged-toothed grimaces. What was once stone was now reptilian skin, the verdant scales glistening as if slimy.

"What did you do to me?"

"I've taken you to the temple like you've asked."

"I mean what's happening to me?"

"All they do takes place behind the scenes."

"Behind the scenes of what?"

"Of the world you know."

Fascination trumped all fear. As a child, he had always liked to watch behind the scenes documentaries that told the story of how his favorite films were made. A peek behind the scenes of the world eclipsed anything he had experienced before.

Beneath his feet, the cobblestone cracked and heaved as if something below was breathing. The clouds above swirled, black in color and set against a fiery red sky. The mansion on the hill had transformed. No longer a piece of Gothic architecture, it had split and twisted into something out of a German Expressionist nightmare, all zigzags, bends, and spirals.

He wondered if he'd followed Marielle into Hell. If so, what waited for him here?

Twenty-Six

They entered the mansion. Red cracks split the walls of the hallway leading from the front door. Light pulsed from them, making fiery haloes in the darkness. The floor shifted and groaned beneath Ward, as if the house stood on unstable ground or that long prophesied earthquake had finally struck Los Angeles. Ward held out his arms to keep his balance.

"What now?" he asked.

"Go to the room where my story was given to you."

"What are you going to do?"

"I'm going with you. My congregation must pay for their apostasy."

• • •

They entered Mr. Whale's crypt of the cinematic dead. Through his new perception, the room had taken on a macabre quality. Theda Bara's eyes in the poster for *Salome* bled thick, black bile down her cheeks. The walls had turned flesh-colored and expanded like a pregnant belly, the life inside rolling and writhing. Torn pages from books and screenplays fluttered through the air like shreds of confetti, the words upon them written in blood-red calligraphy. Actors and actresses on the covers of DVDs and VHSs spoke garbled gibberish through shredded, oozing lips. A fecal smell choked the air.

Marielle walked to the *Salome* poster and tore it down, exposing a vertical slit in the wall. She pressed her hands on either side, pressed her face forward. She licked its edges, rubbed her face against it, kissed it. It expanded, leaking clear mucus. She continued to lick, massaged the sides of it with her hands. Flaps of skin grew out along the edges of the slit, embraced Marielle's head and shoulders.

The slit parted, and Marielle dove between its lips. A throaty moan reverberated in the air of the room. As Marielle disappeared inside, her faint voice called to him. He went up to the crevice, held his breath, and attempted to crawl inside.

It resisted, tightening around the edges. He looked the wet hole up and down, recalled how Marielle had gotten through. He bent forward and ran his tongue along its edges. The discharge had the consistency of honey and tasted like white wine. Its fragrance overpowered the fecal stench in the room as the lips opened wider, the flaps of skin again protruding to wrap around Ward's head. He crawled into the sweet darkness.

The slick walls pressed against him, encircled him with incredible warmth as he inched forward. Blinded by darkness, he moved by feel. Some parts of the passage constricted, and he struggled to get through them. In others, he could almost stand and walk.

The channel grew wider and spilled out into a dark chamber lit by a single blue orb suspended in the air. Across the room, Rachel hung from a cross.

•••

"Rachel!"

She lifted her head to look at him, and a coughing fit overtook her. Purple bruises clouded the skin around her eyes. Barbed wire secured her hands and feet to the planks, dug crimson grooves into her flesh. Droplets of blood flecked the floor.

He stepped forward. Chants filled the room. He called for Marielle, but she was nowhere to be found. He reached for his gun. He hoped there would be less than six cult members.

The walls illuminated like wraparound movie screen. Each panel showed something different. On one, a man repeatedly smashed a hi-def video camera into his head, laughing as his nose and lips gushed blood. On another, a man impaled on a mic stand flailed. The microphone jutted out from between his shattered teeth. On a third, Marielle kissed a young female executive dressed in a tan suit. The woman's hair fell out with bloody pieces of scalp, skin wrinkling and turning gray. More macabre images played along the wall: burnings, slashings, and strangulations. A collage of snuff cinema. All the while, the voices chanted.

He aimed the gun at the sound. Two hooded figures emerged from a dark hall between two screens. Each of them led a line of at least five more. The lines parted and faced each other. From between them came another cloaked figure, wearing a red robe while the others wore black.

The figure in red pulled a curved blade and held it in the air. It glimmered in the blue light.

"Marielle, please, where are you?"

The figure in red brought the knife down and held it at his side. With his other hand, he removed the hood. Ward's chest clenched at the sight of the man beneath the hood.

The hair had gone gray, the eyes sunken back a bit farther, but Ward recognized his father.

His thin lips stretched into a tight smile. "Hello, son."

Stephen Ward stepped aside. A pale hand grabbed one of the hooded men and pulled him into the darkness. A choked scream followed, then nothing. Marielle.

Another hooded man fell away, bellowing. The gravelly sound of breaking bone echoed in the chamber. Ward's father stood stat-

ue-still, even as his followers glanced around in panic. Even as Marielle pounced on another and stole his life with her kiss.

Stephen's smile spread, revealing yellow teeth filed into points. Three hooded figures tackled Marielle to the ground, punching and kicking her. One pulled a knife, stabbed her once, twice. The second man took a knife of his own and raised it over his head. Each brought their blade down, one after the other. Marielle cried out in agony. The third man stomped her.

All the while, the violent imagery played on the surrounding screens, repeating the works of the curse. At least, that was what Ward assumed they were. Some of the footage was in black and white, some of it jerky and silent, others in varying quality of colors from various eras of cinema. *Marielle isn't the first. How long has this curse been active? How many different ghosts trapped in how many different screenplays?*

Marielle rolled out from under her attackers and stood. She moved with grotesque grace, twisting and flipping through the air, tearing out throats, punching through torsos, kissing and stealing life force. She tore the heart from one man's chest, devoured it in two bites. With each kill, she grew stronger, more savage.

The last man tried to run, but she took him by the testicles and pulled them free. She tossed them to the ground, making Ward glad she didn't eat them, and punched into the man's face. Her fist burst out the other side, splattering chunks of brain and skull.

Ward examined the dead. The businessman, Atkins, and Mr. Whale were among them. All of them had belonged to his father's brotherhood.

Marielle turned to the red hooded man. Blood smeared her face, and her eyes had gone deep red. She approached Stephen and attempted to throw a chokehold around him.

She cried out and doubled over, backing away. She tried again, but wailed again and fell back. Stephen faced her. Her features twisted. Ward saw something there that he didn't expect: fear.

"You can't hurt me," Stephen said. "As the Elder, I've orchestrated it so that if you come near me, if you try to hurt me, you'll die. Besides, would you really want to hurt me after all we've shared? After all I've given you?"

Marielle coughed black blood, wiped it away with a trembling claw. Stephen walked past her to where Rachel hung. He held the knife out in front of her. Ward leveled the gun at his father.

"Don't move. You were never a father to me, asshole, so I won't have any second thoughts about wasting you."

Stephen faced his son. "And just how have I never been a father to you? Everything that's led you here has been orchestrated by me. Of course, I didn't do everything. I needed you to make the right moves, and so far, you have."

"The right moves for what?"

"It's time for a new god to rise, and with the new god comes a new congregation. I won't shed any tears for Marielle's victims behind me because this was all part of the plan. My intent is to replace her with Rachel, and for you to be the first of the new congregation. When I die, you'll be an elder, and you can do this all over again."

Rachel squirmed in position and moaned. Ward winced at the agony in it.

"You can end her pain, William. See, the only reason she's still alive is because I need you to kill her."

"Well, fuck you if you think that's gonna happen." Ward squeezed the trigger. Goopy bile dripped out of the tip, but no bullet.

He examined the gun.

"Props like that won't work here. We're behind the scenes, re-member? In the unreal behind the real."

Ward stared at his father. Tears stung his eyes. Marielle hadn't gotten off her knees. Ward could hear her ragged breaths from across the chamber.

"Now, as I said, if you kill her, you'll end her pain. When she returns, she'll become something so much greater. We'll write her story, some poor filmmaker will come along to shoot it, and she'll be the boogeyman for a generation."

"I don't fucking care. It's not gonna happen."

"Rachel, did you hear that, sweetie? Your lover wants you to suffer." Stephen turned and cut a shallow wound along the bottom of her ribcage. Her cry was prolonged and raw. "I know you're ca-pable of killing, William. Having Dalton killed was one step from doing the killing yourself."

Rachel gagged. "What?"

"And you didn't tell her?" He took Rachel's hair in his fist. "Marielle saw your boyfriend's dirty little thoughts and acted on his behalf."

"I didn't want him to die. I was just angry."

His protest did no good. Rachel wept. Stephen cut into her again, and she sobbed.

"Stop it."

"Only you can do that," Stephen said and licked the blood that ran from the wound in her belly. She writhed against his tongue and the bloody slime trail it left. "So, what's it going to be? How long will you let her suffer?"

Ward dropped the gun and held up his hands. "Just stop it. You're ... you're sure she'll come back?"

"Centuries-old rituals aren't going to just stop working. So long as there's a congregation, the power will be there."

Ward stared at his father, digesting what he had just heard.

"Yes, hundreds of years. We used to use plays for this, but no one goes to the theater anymore." Stephen set the curved blade down at Rachel's feet and stepped back. He gestured at the violent images on the screens. "But everyone watches movies. Now do it."

Rachel groaned and pulled against her restraints. Stephen pulled another knife from his cloak. He held its point out and said, "I don't want to kill you, son, but if you try cutting her loose, I won't hesitate."

Ward padded forward. No plan would formulate in his mind. Could he pick up the blade and use it on his father first? Marielle could be no help. If she got so much as a few feet from his father, she would be torn apart.

He took the blade and gazed up at Rachel's dark eyes.

"I didn't kill Dalton, but I'm sorry I didn't tell you he was dead." She shut her eyes, opened them again. He wondered how conscious she was. "I love you. I'm so fucking sorry."

Ward raised the knife and ran at his father.

● ● ●

They collided, exacerbating Ward's injuries, and crashed to the floor with Ward on top. He drove down the knife, but his father caught his wrist and countered. Ward snatched Stephen's forearm with his free hand.

They stayed locked in position, each man trying to gain leverage, each man trying to advance the point of his blade. Ward's father smelled like ash and smoke, like he'd spent the last several years standing next to a raging fire. Or like he' walked out of Hell.

The men grunted as they pushed against each other, exerting everything they had, equally matched in strength. Ward was surprised by how strong his elderly father was. *It's like he's kept up a regimen in the years since faking his death. Like he's been training for this very moment.*

Stephen thrust his head forward, connecting with Ward's. Ward lost momentum. *My father* would *be a dirty fighter.* Another head butt, Ward rolled to the side. His father was upon him in half a second.

He slashed wildly. Ward kept his blade up to block the blows, but some cuts connected with flesh, igniting new wounds in his hand and forearm. He kicked forward, catching his father in the stomach, knocking the older man backwards.

Stephen Ward landed on his ass, sat on the ground, eyes full of rage. Ward charged him, kicked the knife out of his father's hand. He sliced. Stephen leaned back, and the blade missed his throat by less than an inch.

Ward drove forward, knife out, point driving toward his father's left eye. Stephen raised his knees, drove his feet into Ward's abdomen.

Ward fell backward. Spun.

The knife entered the soft flesh beneath Rachel's rib cage. Ward saw what he'd done and screamed.

●●●

She rose. Pain spread through her like a virus. Whatever spell her former lover used was effective. *If she comes near him, it will kill her.* She searched the dark annals of her soul and found she didn't care. To hell with immortality; only revenge mattered to her now.

Ward stared at the knife imbedded in his lover's side. His hands trembled.

His father rose to his feet and grinned.

Marielle approached.

Ward released the blade, stepped back.

"Rachel, oh God, Rachel."

Stephen looked at the bloody heap of his fallen men. He picked up his knife and walked toward his son. Marielle is on his heels. She cried out as pain flared through her.

She fought through it, drew closer; this time the threat of death didn't deter her. Stephen faced her, eyes wide. His mouth opened to say something, but he remained silent.

Her flesh began to tear. Bile rose in her throat. She coughed it out, kept going.

Stephen backed away.

"No! Stay back!"

She reached for him, her hands no more than sinew and blood-stained bone. Her fingers dug into the sides of his face, peeling the flesh from his cheeks. He stabbed into her abdomen with the knife. Still she came. She opened her mouth and placed her lips over his.

She sucked in his energy as her life force bled away. He writhed and gurgled. Blood and flaps of skin fell from her back. Something inside of her split open, spewing tentacles from her chest that encircled her victim and assisted with the feed.

When it was over, she fells to the floor.

The last thing she saw was the blue orb shining delicate light in the darkness.

•••

Ward unwrapped the barbed wire and lowered Rachel down from the cross. He wasn't medically trained, had no idea if he should pull the blade out. Her pain-contorted face stared at him, tears and yellow gunk in her eyes. He took hold of her hand and squeezed.

Behind him, the remains of Marielle and his father oozed and sizzled.

"I'm sorry ... about everything."

"Just forget it. Too late now."

"Rachel, please."

She coughed. Blood bubbled from between her lips.

He cradled her head. "Rachel ..."

Her eyes rolled back. She expelled a prolonged ragged breath.

"Rachel!"

She didn't breathe again.

Twenty-Seven

Ward surveyed the death around him. The effects of Marielle's kiss had mostly worn off. The chamber had transformed, now just a dingy cellar with cinder block walls and cobwebs. Dusty projection screens stood at various locations, but nothing played on them.

Only death remained. His father's followers lay in crumpled, bloody heaps. Marielle and Stephen Ward's soggy bones lay in a pool of pus and liquefied flesh. Rachel lay at his feet, eyes half-open, not breathing. Like in film, the actions that took place behind the scenes directly impacted the film, impacted life.

He shook with the after effects of the battle with his father. With the trauma of everything that had transpired since he put *Mania* into production. He rose to his feet, every joint and muscle protesting, and checked for a way out.

On one end of the basement, a staircase led up to a heavy wood door. He limped up the passage. By the time he reached the halfway point, he couldn't tell between his groans and those from the stairs. By the time he reached the door, he thought he would collapse. He leaned against the wood, breathing heavily, coughing on snot and tears.

The police would want to speak to him, especially after he broke out of prison, especially after they found all these bodies in Mr. Whale's basement. He hoped there would be enough evidence in this house to implicate his father and the brotherhood's involvement in everything. Hoped there would be enough to clear his name.

Hope. What a load of shit.

He worked up the will to open the door and go forward. He emerged in Mr. Whale's crypt of lost cinematic artifacts. The room displayed none of the animation it had behind the scenes. Ward wondered if whatever he needed for evidence would be in here. He thought about looking himself, then stopped when his eyes rested on a video camera that sat on a tripod in the corner.

It was an older model, digital camcorder from the late 90s. He had shot many student films on such a device back in high school and his first year of college. He walked up to it, examined its angles and buttons. Without thinking too much about it, his finger came to rest on the power button. A green light switched on. The camera had power.

Ward swiped it from the tripod and walked back into the basement. Once below, he pressed record.

"This is where it happened," he said. "This is where the actress Rachel Katayama, the woman I loved, was killed."

He did a slow deliberate pan across the basement. The shot came to rest on the cross with its barbed wire hanging from it like a torture porn Easter decoration. He lowered the camera.

"I can't do this."

He thought of Marielle, how her story had taken so many lives, caused so much chaos, how the curse had ultimately enslaved her. Could he bring himself to carry on the tradition? To bring in a new curse? Could he do to Rachel what her father had done to Marielle?

He turned the camera off, collapsed to his knees, sobbing.

Rachel stirred.

It was too late to turn back.

He switched the camera back on as she rose to her feet. She looked at Ward and grinned. He zoomed in, panned from her feet all the way up to her face. Blood soaked her clothes. Her eyes had gone silver. Her skin lost its tone and became gray with death. She moved in jerky, slow strides.

"Hello, Bill."

She came closer. He kept filming, knowing his actions immortalized her. Maybe she would be bound to the curse, but at least she would be alive. At least she wouldn't fade from existence before she had a chance to shine.

Rachel faced him, snatched the camera and turned it on him.

"Are you scared?" she asked.

Ward nodded.

She cocked her head to the side, a strand of blood dribbled from her ear. "Good. You'll taste better that way."

She dropped the camera. It hit the floor with a dull thud. Ward tried to run, but too late. She took hold of the sides of his face, closed her mouth around his. In the arms of Rachel, the new mother of ghosts, he hoped the same immortality would embrace him.

But there was only pain.

THE END

Hollywood Blood and Guts

Somebody finally did it. They found their way around the curse and told the story of *Mania*. Well, more or less. *Mother of Ghosts* was a documentary about the script, the troubled attempts to produce it, and the lore surrounding it. Tonight was the premiere. Julian swore to himself he wouldn't go. He'd refused the filmmakers' requests for interviews. Muted any references to it on social media. Last week, he'd told his friends Patton and Stanley *no fucking way* when they asked if he wanted a ticket. They even brought up his part in one of the more recent aborted productions.

You're right, he'd said. *And I managed to escape unscathed. I'm not fucking that up.*

Indeed, he believed associating with that screenplay in any way, shape, or form would be akin to running *back* into a burning building. And for no good reason. Not to save a child or a pet or an old lady. Just to watch the flames up close. Catch a whiff of smoky air as his flesh burned.

No fucking way.

Of course, that was before he'd seen the photo on Barbara's Instagram tonight.

She and a couple other women were standing in front of the Starland Theater's dark windowed facade, arms around each other and smiling with the sort of enthusiasm some people would pay thousands of dollars to bottle. On the marquee, in black letters, it read, *Mother of Ghosts: The Story of Mania*. When he saw the photo, he squeezed dents into his can of PBR, bolted upright in his pleather armchair, and stared in disbelief, blinking over and over, willing the image to change somehow, or to disappear altogether. But like the ghostly image that had prompted him to run away from that doomed production five years ago—Marielle masturbating with her own intestines—remained in his mind's eye, this troubling image remained on his phone.

Beer fizz spilled over his fingers and jolted him out of his hypnosis. He set down the can and dialed Barbara's number. He thought about texting, since she hated talking on the phone, but decided a phone call would tell her this was something serious.

The call went straight to voicemail.

A full voicemail, undoubtedly clogged with digitally recorded spam.

Fuck.

He texted her.

CALL ME RIGHT AWAY.

Then he called again. No one answered.

Shit. Shit. Shit.

Julian pulled on some pants and grabbed his keys from the TV stand. He opened his knife drawer and saw nothing he could easily conceal. Not like a knife would do him any good. His only hope was to get her and the others out of that theater before the movie started.

He had half an hour.

When he arrived in the vicinity, the line, which was wrapped around the block, had already begun to move forward. He pulled over in a fire lane, put on his flashers, and got out. Up ahead, the line proceeded to the entrance. A beefy bouncer checked tickets. Julian jogged by the patrons, looking for Barbara and the other two girls, whose names he couldn't quite remember. Maybe one was Meg, *maybe*. He didn't see their faces anywhere. Halfway down the line, he started calling Barbara's name. Probably sounded and looked half-crazy, but he didn't give a shit. Everyone attending this premiere was in danger. Although the making of the film itself had caused no strife, it could be the ghost was just biding her time. Gathering her strength.

It gave him a bad feeling.

"What the fuck is wrong with this guy?" he heard someone ask.

"Hey, dude," another said. "Meth kills."

"Should I call the police?" a woman muttered.

Julian stopped, spun on his heel.

"Yes," he said. "Call the police. Call them now."

The woman he presumed had asked the question scrunched up her brow in confusion.

"Are you deaf?" he asked. "Call the cops. If someone doesn't cancel this show, you're all going to die."

Several people murmured. One bro-type derisively said, "This fucking guy."

No one nearby looked like Barbara. He stared at Police Lady.

"What are you waiting for? Call them."

Police Lady put a phone to her ear. The woman beside her forced her to lower it.

"He's fine. Just a druggie." Then, to Julian. "Go rape a raccoon, you back alley bum."

What a bitch, he thought. *I don't look homeless.*

"Hey, you got some kind of a problem?"

In his periphery, he saw the bouncer coming toward him, fists balled.

Shit.

Julian had never been in a proper fight, save for some play-ground scuffles back in elementary school. He didn't want to start now, but he would if saving Barbara depended on it. He faced the oncoming bouncer.

Even if I'm guaranteed to get my ass kicked.

Dude towered over him.

"What's the trouble, guy?" the bouncer asked.

"I just ..." Julian grimaced. "I'm looking for someone."

"Yeah? Got a ticket?"

"Look, I just need ..."

"Ticket or not?"

"Well, no, but ..."

"Then fuck off, guy."

"What? No!"

The bouncer stepped closer, loomed over Julian. He smelled like Axe Body Spray and cheap bourbon. Probably Old Crow.

"Really, guy?"

Julian decided to take a rare risk. He closed the gap between himself and the bouncer.

"I'm just looking for my girlfriend. *Guy.*"

The bouncer scowled at Julian. Then smiled, showing big, white teeth.

Hey, Julian thought, *maybe I earned his respect.*

The bouncer shoved Julian onto his ass. To add insult to injury, Julian landed in a black puddle. The filthy water soaked him to his underwear. It felt, smelled, and looked like something a rat would use for a bathtub.

"Goddamn it. What the hell?"

"Told you to fuck off."

"*Julian?*"

Barbara's voice came from somewhere behind him. Though glad he wasn't too late, he hated for her to see him in his current state. He scooted back from the imposing bouncer and staggered to his feet.

"What happened?" she asked, glancing between both men.

The two women with her whispered something to each other.

"You know him?" the bouncer asked.

Barbara took Julian's arm, helped him steady himself.

"What's going on?" asked one of Barbara's friends, the one he thought was Meg.

Everyone was watching. Some of them were filming with their phones. Julian had little doubt he'd see himself on YouTube tomorrow. *Unhinged Meth-head Tries to Crash Movie Premiere, Pisses Pants Instead*, the title would read.

"Does he have a ticket?" asked the other. She was always dressed to the nines and wearing a top hat. Tonight was no exception. He had no clue what her name was.

"At this point, it doesn't matter," the bouncer said. "Soaked as he is, I'm not about to let him sit in one of our seats. Besides, he pissed me off."

"Oh, come off it, Ted," Top Hat said. The bouncer reddened. She took Julian's arm, too. "A few minutes in front of the hand dryer will fix him up good."

"Is the show sold out?" Maybe Meg asked.

The bouncer's smugness returned. He met Julian's gaze. "Yep. Guess you that means you'll have to kick rocks, *guy*."

Desperate now, Julian turned to Barbara. "Barb, please. You can't go in there."

"Why not?" she asked. Then, as if just now remembering his part in the previous, failed production. "Oh."

"He doesn't really think ..." Maybe Meg trailed off.

"Of course he doesn't," Top Hat said. She frowned at Barbara. "Does he?"

"Time's up, guy. I gotta get these people inside."

"Barbara, don't."

"We already have tickets. It's going to be fine, I promise."

He shook his head. She released his arm.

"I'll call you afterward."

"No," he reached for her.

Ted blocked him. His hand brushed the bouncer's chest. Ted leaned down to put his mouth next to Julian's ear.

"You better get a move on. I don't want to beat your ass in front of your girl, but I will if you push me."

Fuming, his fists now clenched, he spun on his heel and walked the other way. Some people in line laughed at him. Others made sarcastic comments. He kept his head down and kept going. His car was behind him. Barbara and her friends were behind him.

About to enter Hell.

Julian would have to go in the back way.

Another bouncer was waiting for him by the fire exit in the dark alley between the Starland and a shuttered bar called The Whiskey Drip. This guy was no less imposing than the first, and he looked even meaner.

"Guy out front said you might show up back here," he drawled, then put his left hand around his right fist and cracked his knuckles. "You best leave."

"Look, man, I don't want any trouble. It's just ... I was involved in the last attempted production of *Mania,* and I'm worried something bad might happen tonight."

"Something bad will happen if you don't get the fuck out of here."

The bouncer took a step forward, then halted mid-stride. Something halfway between a croak and a gag came from his throat. His eyes and a large vein in his forehead bulged. He reached forward, hands grasping the air, his mouth moving but forming no words—nothing audible anyway, and Julian was no lipreader.

Julian watched with part morbid fascination and part creeping dread. At first, he thought the bouncer might be having a seizure, but he knew better. What he feared was coming true right before his eyes. Marielle was here. She'd been waiting for this night, and now the carnage would begin. He wanted to turn and run, but he couldn't leave Barbara and her friends behind. No way could he let them—all those people—die. Knowing what he knew, it'd be akin to murder. But maybe this wasn't what he thought. Maybe it was just a seizure or some other medical condition.

With a wet squelch, a red rose of blood blossomed across the bouncer's chest. It almost looked like a gunshot wound, but Julian heard no report, and the only other person in this alley was him. He wasn't armed. The bouncer's arms fell limp to his sides. A third arm punched through the bloody hole, holding a gristly lump of meat. The hand opened its fingers and dropped the heart to the asphalt before extracting itself and leaving the bouncer to fall twitching beside the organ.

"Oh, *fuck*!" Julian backpedaled, his own heart feeling like it might burst like a water balloon. "Holy fucking shit!"

The bouncer's murderer stepped from the shadows.

It wasn't who Julian expected.

"*Rachel?*"

"Not anymore," she said with a sinister grin.

The girlfriend of William Ward, doomed director of the last production, the one Julian had left, stood over the dead man. Blood covered her right arm to the elbow and dripped from her fingers. She'd disappeared sometime after a fire on the set halted production indefinitely. Now, it seemed she'd somehow replaced Marielle as Mania's earthly vessel.

A tangle of tendrils snaked from beneath her skirt. She opened her mouth, revealing daggerlike teeth, and loosed a tongue that looked like it might be covered in warts.

Julian yelped, not giving a shit how he sounded. What little delusions of his toughness remained after his humiliating encounter with Ted dissolved in a matter of seconds. He spun on his heel to run, but instead came face to face with Rachel or Mania or whatever this fiend now called herself. The alley was a dead end, and there would be no getting past this awful ghost. He could only enter the theater, even knowing the chances it would provide sanctuary were slim to none.

He ran the other way, leaping over the now still corpse of the bouncer and grabbing hold of the exit door. A sign warned an alarm would sound, but maybe that's what he needed to happen to save Barbara, to save himself, to save everybody. He yanked open the door, but no alarm went off.

And Rachel was coming closer.

In a snap decision, he ducked into the theater and slammed the door behind him. He turned, expecting the ghost to be waiting, but no one was there. A dimly lit hallway stretched before him, lined with posters for old B movies and glass cabinets containing film reels. At the opposite end, he saw the line of people filing into the auditorium showing *Mother of Ghosts*.

"No, don't!" he yelled and tromped toward the crowd.

The first bouncer, Ted, cut him off.

"Well, well, well. I was kind of hoping you'd turn back up. Not sure how you got past Ramsey, but you're not gonna get past me."

Ted came forward. In desperation, and without even really thinking about it, Julian reared back and kicked the bouncer in the nuts. Ted doubled over and then tipped to the side, muttering something about bashing in Julian's face.

Julian barely heard it. He just kept running. The auditorium door closed behind the last in line and Julian opened it.

But something was very wrong.

The entryway was empty, the auditorium quiet. Something he couldn't quite make out played on the screen, but there was no sound, and the film quality was grainy. He stepped into the auditorium. Every seat was empty, too. The place was not just vacant, it was significantly depreciated. Material was peeled back or rubbed off from all the chairs. Some had their stuffing spilling from slashes. The whole place smelled like spilled soda, old butter, and rancid piss. The only sounds were Julian's tentative footsteps on the dirty, sticky floor.

He glanced around and tried to make sense of everything. His gaze drifted to the screen.

The picture showed a full movie auditorium. His panic surged as he scanned the faces for Barbara and her friends. Somehow, the silence in the theater made everything much worse. The voices in his head telling him he never should've come, that his girlfriend was dead and he was next were all the louder now.

Then he spotted her, and Maybe Meg, and Top Hat.

But they were on the screen. He was in this strange, abandoned place.

This haunted place from which all his nightmares emanated.

An angry, red fire ignited in the bottom left corner of the screen. It didn't take long to spread like spilled liquid. The flames surrounded the people on the screen, who appeared blissfully unaware they were burning to death. Julian ran to the nearest exit, but this door—unlike the others, which had opened and led him to this, his ultimate doom—didn't open.

There was more fire than screen now. It consumed Barbara and her friends last. Taunting Julian as he screamed unheeded, unheard warnings. This fire had consciousness. It had intentions, because *she* had brought it. She who now wore Rachel's face. She who now stood before him again, now mere kissing distance away. Her whited out eyes met his. Her skin was smooth but too pale, too blue.

Awful realization settled over him. She had drawn him out tonight. The others were never in danger. This was about unfinished business.

"Why now?" he asked.

"Why not?"

Rachel took him by the throat. Her fingernails dug into his jugular, and she swallowed his gurgling screams with a noxious kiss of death.

About The Author

Lucas Mangum is the multiple award-nominated author of *Saint Sadist*, as well as *Gods of the Dark Web, Mania,* and the collection *Engines of Ruin*. He lives in Austin with his family. For more information, visit lucasmangum.com or follow him on Twitter @RealLucasMangum